THE GOLDE

THE GOLDEN HOURS

A Literary Salon's Anthology II

EDINBURGH
LITERARY
SALON

-m-
MERCHISTON PUBLISHING
www.merchistonpublishing.com

First published in 2023 by
Merchiston Publishing
www.merchistonpublishing.com
in collaboration with
Edinburgh Literary Salon
www.edinburghliterarysalon.org
With the help of MSc Publishing students at Edinburgh Napier University
Editorial: Megan Lewis & Natalie Quinn (Editorial Team Leaders)
Joanna Das, Natalie Ellis, Kate Lally, Lisa Lavelle, Ciara Marr,
Jacob Stewart-Kellett & Emily Turner
Marketing: Karley Dajka, Elizabeth Smith

Foreword © J. A. Sutherland, *pp* Edinburgh Literary Salon
Britta Benson *Family Gatherings*, Mary Byrne *A Day in November*, Ash Caton
Hutton's Section, Philip Caveney *Numbered*, Anna Cheung *The Watching*,
Julie Galante *Alternative Lifestyle*, Allan Gaw *The Bus Stop at Armageddon*,
June Gemmell *Ypres*, Pippa Goldschmidt *Here Lived*, Naomi Head *Kitchen Love,
part one*, Fiona Herbert *Gathering*, Stuart Johnstone *Bone China*, Musenga Katongo
When the Poets Gather, Mark Lewis *Lavender and Death*, Marcas Mac an Tuairneir
Antebellum, Kirsty MacDonald *Haematology Day Unit*, Kirsten MacQuarrie *Agnes*,
Roddie McKenzie *Gathering for Adventure*, David McVey *He Fell Among Stories*,
Ricky Monahan Brown *Praying to the Resurrector*, Chiamaka Okike *A Name No
Mother Would Give You*, Mary Paulson-Ellis *The Cruet Set*, Alycia Pirmohamed
Once, You Gathered in My Arms, Lizzie Smith *Tale of a Tail*, Tracey S. Rosenberg
Four Cups, Charlie Roy *By the Light of Brìghde*, Catherine Simpson *Exotic Fiona*,
Suzanne Smith *Church After Lockdown*, Thomas Stewart *Spoon*, Rosie Sumsion
Spell for Comfort, Augustijn van Gaalen *The Fisherfolk of Rakhine*

ISBN: 978-1-911524-04-5

Printed by Bell & Bain Ltd, Glasgow, G46 7UQ
Typeset in Adobe Caslon Pro 12/14pt

Contents

DUSK

DAWN

Acknowledgements

W e are grateful to the following organisations and individuals for all their work and support to help us produce *The Golden Hours*, our second anthology.

The Edinburgh Literary Salon Steering Group.

Edinburgh UNESCO City of Literature.

Baillie Gifford.

Avril Gray and the student volunteers from the MSc Publishing programme (2022/23) at Edinburgh Napier University: Joanna Das, Natalie Ellis, Kate Lally, Lisa Lavelle, Megan Lewis, Ciara Marr, Natalie Quinn, Jacob Stewart-Kellett and Emily Turner (Editorial team), and Karley Dajka and Elizabeth Smith (Marketing team).

Katya Bacica for administrating all submissions, and for her editorial work.

Elise Carmichael for the cover (and bookmarks).

The submissions judging panel: Ali Bowden, Avril Gray, Rebecca Heap, Stuart Johnstone, Madeleine Mankey, Eleanor Pender, and John Stoddart.

The contributors: Britta Benson, Mary Byrne, Ash Caton, Philip Caveney, Anna Cheung, Augustijn van Gaalen, Julie Galante, Allan Gaw, June Gemmell, Pippa Goldschmidt, Naomi Head, Fiona Herbert,

Stuart Johnstone, Musenga Katongo, Mark Lewis, Marcas Mac an Tuairneir, Kirsty MacDonald, Kirsten MacQuarrie, Roddie McKenzie, David McVey, Ricky Monahan Brown, Chiamaka Okike, Mary Paulson-Ellis, Alycia Pirmohamed, Tracey S. Rosenberg, Charlie Roy, Catherine Simpson, Lizzie Smith, Suzanne Smith, Thomas Stewart, and Rosie Sumsion.

Last, but not least, The Outhouse Bar who made us so welcome as we emerged from pandemic lockdowns.

Foreword

There's a sign outside an Edinburgh primary school that says 'NO GATHERING' – an odd hangover from the pandemic, and yet it's still here in 2023. It seems hard to believe that, only two years ago, we were tentatively planning a significant gathering of our own: the first in-person Literary Salon since lockdowns began, to launch our first anthology, *Lost, Looking & Found*. A Literary Salon's Renaissance indeed!

Finding a suitable venue, preferably one with an open-air option since the world was still being cautious about the dreaded virus, was a difficult task. Fortunately, we found The Outhouse, tucked away on Broughton Street Lane, with an outside courtyard and lots of umbrellas just in case. Thankfully, those umbrellas proved redundant: the weather was perfect, allowing us to come together and launch our first book in front of a great crowd of friends. We even had fireworks!

Well, sparklers anyway.

As a bonus, The Outhouse then became a new home for the Salon. Our regular events have been held in the upstairs Function Room and – a legacy from Covid – livestreamed on Zoom, enabling us to expand our audience and connect with friends both near and far.

Lost, Looking & Found was our first anthology, but we wondered if it would be a one-off project. You'll have gathered, holding this lovely book in your hands, that a second anthology was planned. We collaborated once more with our friends at Edinburgh Napier University and their postgraduate publishing course, and we set the wheels in motion to publish again with their imprint, Merchiston Publishing.

Questions arose. If the theme of the first book was 're-birth', what should the next be? Suckers for etymology, we looked into the Greek origins of the word 'anthology' (an'θɒlədʒi), which is defined as a collection of poems or other pieces of writing. Coming from anthologia – a combination of anthos, ('flower') and logia, 'collection' (from legein 'gather') – the word literally means 'a gathering of flowers'.

'Gathering' was therefore chosen as our theme. What, then, is the background of gathering?

Tam O' Shanter and Souter Johnnie 'getting fou and unco happy' while poor Kate was 'gathering her brows like gathering storm.' Clouds and wrath: the stuff of Scottish weather. There's the Highland Gatherings, or the Gaelic Mòd (and we're delighted to have a Gaelic contribution in this book) bringing people together through tradition, sport, and culture.

Here in the Central Belt, eighteenth-century gatherings occurred increasingly over tea, and taverns, clubs, and associations became new melting-pots of ideas and discussions, ushering in The Scottish Enlightenment. In Libberton's Wynd, many writers, philosophers, and artists – Fergusson, Scott, Hume, Burns – would gather in John Dowie's Tavern for discussion and disputation, fuelled in equal measure by ale and intellect. A blueprint for successive Literary Salons.

Edinburgh likes a blether as well as a hearty debate. Burghers have a propensity for a good old moan too. Twenty-two years ago, whether we loved or loathed the New Parliament building, the contention was that it was designed without a proper brief – or perhaps because the architect was a single male Catalan. Now, mostly forgotten. Then was the undeniable farce of The Tram. Or will outrage lessen now we can tram all the way to Newhaven?

Now there's another divisive blot on the horizon, dominating our city's skyline: architectural marmite if ever there was. Locals do not call the St James' Hotel a Walnut Whip; it's known as the Golden Turd. Whether you like it or hate it, you cannae polish it. But as a wise person said, you can roll it in glitter.

This restless multiplicity, Edinburgh's argumentative nature, is part of our city's famous Jekyll & Hyde duality. It's two sides of a coin. But it's a golden coin.

These are disputatious days, but while it's easy to denigrate, there's also much to celebrate. Art and literature, debate and discourse, bringing people together, breaking down barriers – these are all at the heart of creativity, and at the heart of Edinburgh Literary Salon. The arts were there for many of us during lockdown, shining some light through a shadowed period of our history. We're used to 'making good' in Scotland... just think of the weather.

We hope that this anthology serves as a continuation of that light, as much as a reflection on the dark. When we were discussing some of the themes flowing through the works collected here, we came across the Japanese art of kintsugi, or 'golden repair': the practise of mending a broken vessel with gold, making it more precious than it was before. What better way to describe the restorative value of art in confusing, uncertain times, when people can feel so far removed from one another.

By collecting the words of the finest writers we knew, and some we didn't but do now, we got so much more than a bunch of flowers. In this gathering of poetry, prose, historical fiction, memoir, and reflection, we struck gold. We're delighted how these writers explored the theme, taking us from darkness into light.

After all, dusk and dawn are moments of uncertainty and acceptance, trepidation and hope, beginnings and endings – the golden hours of in-between. We're looking forward to what's on the horizon.

DUSK

ONCE, YOU GATHERED IN MY ARMS

Alycia Pirmohamed

Everything I love has a name –
so what to call this?

'A tube of lipstick lost under the porch.'

Or maybe I'll call it proximity: the dove
drifting on the surface
   of her own reflection,

the distance between the first stone
and the first woman,

and dark hair parted
   exactly in the middle. I'll call it:

'the moon has forgotten how to speak'

or 'kissing a bee-stung mouth.'

How else to disclose the petals
of my memory?
   Every hallucination slipping back

and forth like a river over my skin.
Two nouns dissolve into the threshold
   of desire,

and on page twenty-seven,
only a few lines of Sappho in the margins.

'Fragments that crush me.'

Alycia Pirmohamed is the author of *Another Way to Split Water*, the pamphlets *Hinge* and *Faces that Fled the Wind*, and the collaborative essay, *Second Memory*, which was co-authored with Pratyusha. She is co-founder of the Scottish BPOC Writers Network, a co-organiser of the Ledbury Poetry Critics, and she currently teaches at the University of Cambridge. Alycia received an MFA from the University of Oregon and a PhD from the University of Edinburgh. In 2020, she was the recipient of the Edwin Morgan Poetry Award.

THE CRUET SET

Mary Paulson-Ellis

When I was just a little girl,
I asked my mother, what will I be?
Will I be pretty? Will I be rich?
Here's what she said to me…

Stop! Let it go.

My mother's voice is sharp. The knife's cry. Her words flow from my mouth unbidden, though my mouth isn't even open. I crouch in the corner of my living room, lips sealed by a strange white dust. In the centre, piled on my carpet – a crate of badly stacked china, a cardboard box scrawled in marker. I watch them come in and go out, the strangers. That young woman with the leggings. The older one with scratches on her arms. They walk about my flat as though they own it, carry my possessions in their hands.

The living room is cold. It clings to me. My petticoat. My shoe. I wait for my mother to speak again. But there is nothing. Nothing here but me.

The woman in the leggings appears with an unclad duvet spilling from a bin bag, adds it to the pile. Why are they even bothering with the duvet, that's what I want to know. The stain is hidden, but it's there, all that life seeping out of me, month after month, nothing left but a faded patch of rust. No one to see me through.

I think of the stain's twin, on the sheet. Of its shadow on the mattress. Will they drag the mattress in here, too? Or tumble it down the communal stair to join the rest of my belongings stacked in front of the garage door – my cooker with the faulty ring, my fridge, inside the half beetroot, that packet of sliced cheese. The garage door is marked with its own stain now. Soot. Lit up by a girl who came in the night not long since, put a match to it, like they'll put a match to me soon. Blue jets, one last blaze. No goodbye but the clank of that small square hatch as they close the oven door. Disintegration. That's what it's all about, what it comes to in the end.

From my place in the corner, I watch as the strangers come in and go out. In the kitchen, I hear the clatter of my Pyrex mixing bowls, my mother's fish slice. The woman with the scratches on her arms deposits something on top of the crate of china, turns to leave. I hear the familiar opening and closing of my front door, the click of the mortice, another day at an end. I peer across the wasteland of my living room. Something returns my stare. Two women and a baby. Salt, Pepper, Mustard Pot. It is the cruet set.

In the kitchen, Lena is alive once more. I can hear her laugh, that smoky bark.

All the lights on, nothing but bare bulbs. I shade my eyes, the overwhelming brightness, squint through the door.

I can see myself in the corner, between the table and the cooker. I am twirling and twirling, a flash of knickers beneath my Christmas frock. Lena sits at the table, hair a dark shimmer, my mother opposite, lips a crimson slash. There is the sticky scent of brandy, a thin curl rising from the ashtray. The cruet set lies abandoned in a crumple of tissue. Two china women, tiny holes piercing their crowns. One fat baby, rosebud cheeks and a notch for the spoon. Lena has brought it from her Spanish holiday. I know I will lean in to touch.

Stop! Let it go.

The knife's cry.

Lena laughs again. Then she sings, *Will we have rainbows, day after day…* I close my eyes, twirl and twirl, bare my knickers to the world. The table rocks. The salt woman falls. Lena steadies the pepper. My mother steadies me. I feel the soft curl of her fingers on my wrist. It is the three of us. It is the three.

That night I unpack everything. Mother's saucers. The coffee pot with the chipped spout. It takes me the whole night, adrift on a sea of crumpled newspaper, till my thumbs are smudged black, till I can't see my shoes. The china spreads about me like a pool.

The night is cold. I am cold, blood freezing in my veins. I drag the duvet from its plastic shroud, wrap it about my shoulders, trail the stain from room to room. I unpack the decorative towel set, the electronic clock. In the bedroom I lie on the bare mattress, match stain to stain. Outside somebody is singing. Inside nothing but that breathing, close in my ear. A kind of labour. A kind of stop start. The last gasp of a child's rattle winding to its end.

When I grew up and fell in love,
I asked my sweetheart, what lies ahead?
Will we have rainbows day after day?
Here's what my sweetheart said...

It is morning, a chill nip, the tips of my fingers a dull sort of blue. I am in the corner once more, lips sealed by a strange white dust. In the middle of my carpet – a crate of badly stacked china, a box scrawled in marker. The woman in the leggings walks across my living room, disappears. I look through the space, searching for the cruet set. But it has vanished. They have repacked everything. I slept too long.

All day they empty me. The towel set from my bathroom. Books I haven't read. The mountain of my belongings ebbs and flows, as the light ebbs and flows, falling across the room in different angles as the sun passes round. By the time it disappears, they have taken down the curtains, lifted the carpet. The older woman scratches and scratches at her arms.

Stop!

Nobody can hear me.

They take everything. Even the underlay.

That night the bare boards of my home are filmed with dust. I press my toes in it, touch my tongue to the floor, watch the damp of my saliva shrink away. Everything is disappearing, that is what I'm thinking. Even me.

Outside I hear it again. Singing. A ragged sort of song. I cleave to the bathroom window frame, watch through the glass. I don't turn on the light. I haven't turned on the light for days now. Better to see in the dark.

There are three of them this time. They have gathered

by the lock-ups, by the garage door with its streak of soot. But they are not the strangers. Not the girl. They are the dispossessed. People left behind, like me. They are waiting, I think, for me to join them in the courtyard. To put a match to my petticoat, perhaps. My shoe. I feel myself thin now, nothing but a splinter, a skelf beneath the skin. They lift their mouths to my window, begin their call.

I feel the pull. But I can't go out yet. I can't. My mother needs me here.

My mother sits in the corner of the living room where I usually crouch, hair yellowed, tiny rivers of crimson bleeding from her lips. She gazes out of the window, across the courtyard, towards the flats opposite. She is looking for Lena. Always looking for Lena. But Lena's place is empty, cleared long ago.

One week, that was all it took, top to bottom, bottom to top. The same amount of time it has taken the strangers to clear me. My mother watched from the window as they did it, one day after the next. All the comings and goings. All the ins and outs. The pile on the pavement that grew and grew. She watched until there was nothing left to see. Then she was gone, vanished from her chair before I realised what was happening, out in front of the lock-ups instead, hands wild, knickers on display.

The car was packed. Boot full, roof-rack covered in tarpaulin. The man stood over my mother, bared his teeth at her as though he was a dog:

Bitch.

She bared hers in return. Then I was on her, dragging her away.

My mother moaned as they drove from the courtyard. Him and Lena. Lena and him. She pressed her soft cheek to the unforgiving glass, whispered:

Lena

In a voice I'd never heard before.

I hated her then, Lena, how she didn't turn her head. Not even once. Nothing but a headscarf, a thin curl of smoke drifting from the car window, then gone.

In my living room, my mother's breath steams the pane, hair yellowed, mouth bleeding into flesh. *What will I do without Lena*, that is what she says, over and over. And I think, *At least you have me.*

> *Now I have children of my own,*
> *They ask their mother, what will I be?*
> *Will I be handsome? Will I be rich?*
> *I tell them tenderly...*

It is night. In the living room, me and my mother. I am wearing my Christmas frock. Her hair gleams. I stand on her toes, she holds my arms. Her breath drifts towards me across the space between us, the sweet scent of brandy. Then we begin to move, a slow dance. The cruet set lies abandoned on the table. It is the two of us. The two.

My mother and I dance until we can't dance anymore. I hold her close, her yellowed hair, her crimson lips. Until I hear it, soft, in my ear – the curlew's night-time cry:

Stop. Let it go.

In the shadow of the bathroom mirror I trace a finger about my lips, admire their lilac tinge. I can sense them in the courtyard – the chorus, their upturned mouths – standing by the garage door. In my head I continue to pace out the dance. I think of the cruet set – Salt. Pepper. Mustard Pot – where it might go next. I could write a note to go with it, some sort of greeting. But I do not have a piece of paper. I do not have a pen. My flat is bare now. In the kitchen, nothing but a scatter of crumbs. In the living room, nothing but dust. They have emptied it, the strangers. From the lampshades to the fridge. From the blinds to the underlay. There is nothing left but me.

Outside, my city sings to me, beckoning me with its song. Inside, bare boards, the cold metal of the mortice waiting to be turned. I stand behind my front door, press waxy fingertips to the wood. It must be dark outside, I think. It must be dark. I am afraid of the dark. But they are waiting for me. Waiting to gather me in.

'Que Sera, Sera (Whatever Will Be, Will Be)' was written by Jay Livingston and Ray Evans. Lyrics: Jay Livingston Music, Inc / Wixen Music Publishing.

Mary Paulson-Ellis writes across the genres of crime, historical, and literary fiction. Her debut novel, *The Other Mrs Walker*, was a *Times* bestseller and Waterstones Scottish Book of the Year. Mary has written for *The Guardian* and BBC Radio 4, and was recently awarded the Dr Gavin Wallace Fellowship, hosted by the Edinburgh UNESCO City of Literature Trust, to write a novel about her home city of Edinburgh. *Emily Noble's Disgrace* is her latest book.

TALE OF A TAIL

Lizzie Smith

And as she combed her hair,
she sang of the treasures she'd
combed from the sands:
a polished mussel shell,
a frond of pink seaweed
pots of periwinkles
glass,
feather of a gull
razor shells
limpets
mask
a ton of stones
old rope
plastic.
But as she crooned
her voice cracked
the mask slipped
and she gasped
at the towering tsunami of
discarded toys:
Barbie limbs
bricks
a bra-less Ariel
from that fairytale –
with a sad ending for the
little
mermaid.

Lizzie Smith is a Scottish wild swimmer, singer, poet, and mother. The haiku influences in her work comes from living in Japan. Her first poetry collection *Mermaid on Legs* was published in 2020. Her work has placed in over twenty national and international poetry competitions and been published in over twenty collections. She is a wordsmith with the Leith Art Collective, WHAT! Appearing locally in the Edinburgh Fringe and further afield, she loves performing her poetry, and has read her mermaid poems at the Edinburgh Literary Salon. Ecopoetry is her mission.

NUMBERED

Philip Caveney

It's a mistake, thought Cam.

It was perhaps the fifteenth time he'd told himself this since his arrest earlier that morning. He sat in the humid interview room where the cops had left him, elbows resting on a grubby formica table. Across from him was an empty chair that appeared to be waiting patiently for somebody to occupy it. Cam's own patience had long since evaporated. Glancing at his watch, he saw that he had been waiting for more than forty minutes.

It didn't help that it was the hottest day in recent memory and there was no air conditioning – or at least, none that worked. Climate disaster, that's what everybody had been saying for years, and now it was forty degrees in mid-April, garden lawns were burned ochre and birds were falling dead from the sky, so clearly, they'd been right. Sweat oozed maddeningly from Cam's pores, ran tickling from his underarms beneath his short-sleeved plaid shirt. His chino trousers were sticking to his thighs.

To his right a mirrored window ran the length of one wall and Cam knew enough from TV crime shows to realise that there were people on the other side of that glass, studying him, commenting on the fact that he was visibly perspiring, an intimation of guilt. He tried to keep his features impassive, wanting to give an impression of innocence, then had to remind himself he had nothing to feel guilty about anyway. He was mystified by what had happened this morning.

The worst thing was that they'd come to his place of work, two young coppers, a man and a woman, sweating in stab proof vests. Thank God they hadn't felt the need to use the handcuffs or electronic batons that dangled threateningly from their utility belts. He'd been in the shared office, quietly inputting data and lamenting the fact that he still had another two years before he hit seventy-five and could claim his state pension. The cops had marched straight up to him, enquired if he was Cameron McCready and, when he'd nodded, they'd lifted him from his chair and frogmarched him straight out of the building, while his workmates looked on in open-mouthed astonishment.

He'd tried asking the cops questions as they drove him the short distance to St Leonard's Street in their battered old electric squad car, but they'd ignored him. Once at police headquarters, they'd bundled him straight through the entrance and along a labyrinth of grubby corridors, until they'd deposited him here. They'd confiscated his phone and left without another word.

What about protocol? Cam asked himself. He appreciated that things were in meltdown now, that the world was rapidly going to hell in a handbasket, but shouldn't he at least have been checked in at the desk? How could this be allowed, left to stew here all alone, without even a glass of water? He was a law-abiding citizen!

His friend, Danny, had seen somebody on the street once and actually mistaken him for Cam, even called out his name only for the man to stare back, mystified. You read about stuff like that in the *Edinburgh Evening News* every night. A case of mistaken identity. Boy, the cops would be so embarrassed when they realised their mistake! Maybe Cam would be able to claim compensation…

A door finally opened, and two men came into the room. The first was a small, skinny man, dressed in a dark suit, which seemed totally inappropriate for the weather. He had a sheen of sweat on his pale features, the flesh taut around his cheek bones. His hair had receded to a few grey wisps plastered to the top of his skull. Cam noticed that he had a manila file tucked under one arm. He pulled out the vacant chair and sat down, then placed the file on the table and opened it. He studied pages of scribbled notes.

The second man was the polar opposite to his companion, though similarly attired. He was tall, broad shouldered and had a smiling, almost cherubic face, his curly red hair abundant but carefully trimmed. He remained standing, his back against a wall, arms crossed over his chest. He studied Cam and his cold blue eyes had an unsettling intensity to them. Cam couldn't hold their gaze, so he directed his opening remark to the man at the table.

'There's been a mistake,' he said.

The man lifted his eyes from the file and gazed calmly at Cam. 'You're not Cameron Mcready?' he murmured.

'Well, yes, I am…'

'Then there's no mistake.' The man went back to his reading.

'That's not what I meant,' insisted Cam. He cleared his throat. 'I haven't done anything wrong. I've no idea why I'm here.'

The man gave a sigh. Again, he raised his gaze to examine Cam, the brown eyes lingering this time, taking him in, assessing him. 'An innocent man,' he said tonelessly. 'What a surprise! You'd be amazed how many we get in here.'

'If somebody could tell me what this is all about?' pleaded Cam. 'Perhaps I could help. I want to help.'

'Very noble of you. Well, Mr Mcready, it's about your little gatherings.'

Cam stared at him. 'My little…' The words did not compute. He considered them for a moment, looking for meaning, but couldn't find any. 'What gatherings?' he asked. 'I'm sorry, you're going to have to help me out here. I'm not trying to be difficult, but I haven't the first idea what you're talking about.'

The man didn't look away. 'Allow me to refresh your memory,' he suggested. 'The last Tuesday of every month. Ring any bells?'

The penny dropped. Cam even gave an involuntary gasp of laughter.

'You're talking about the meetings!' he exclaimed. 'With my friends.' Again, he couldn't stop himself from laughing at the ridiculousness of it.

'You find this amusing?' murmured the man.

'No,' said Cam, hastily. 'Of course not. It's just… those gatherings, as you call them, are completely harmless.'

'Really? So tell me about them.'

'There's not much to tell. Just me and three old pals, people I've known all my life. We meet in this little room above…'

'... the Outhouse,' said the man. 'And you've been meeting there for the past eight months. With these men.' He slid a sheet of paper across the desk so Cam could see it. Three familiar names, written in neat capital letters, and underlined so there could be no mistake.

Now Cam felt bewildered all over again. 'It's surely not a crime to meet with friends for a drink and a chat!' he protested.

'That would depend,' said the man, 'on what you're chatting about.'

Cam had to think about it, sifting through the various bits of nonsense that constituted a typical meeting of his little group. 'We talk about all kinds of things. What's in the news, what's on the telly, who we've met, who we haven't seen in ages. Mostly we discuss trains.'

The man stared. 'Trains?' he echoed.

'Yes. We're trainspotters. You know, proper old-fashioned trainspotters. We look for different locomotives and note down the chassis numbers. We used to do it when we were kids; it was a passion back then. More recently, after my wife died...' Cam paused so the man could offer his condolences but that didn't happen, so he continued 'I was feeling at a loose end. Trying to make sense of my life, what it's become. Just... dull routine. I always thought I'd be retired by now but obviously the government has other ideas.'

'And you resent that, do you?'

'No! It's just the way of the world. Anyway, one night, the four of us were in the Outhouse, having a pint after work, and I asked them if they remembered trainspotting when we were lads.' He smiled, wistfully. 'Weekends, mostly. We'd go out after breakfast, get ourselves up to some vantage point where we had a clear view, and we'd spend the day noting down the numbers.'

'Hmm.'

'Yes. Every engine has one painted on its chassis. Of course, back then it was very different. You might still see the occasional steam train. Remember them? Hard to recall now, I know, but oh, the majesty of them! The sound, the smell…You can still find the odd one, but they're mostly for tourists these days. I realised it wouldn't be quite the same as when we were kids, but we were so bored and there are still trains. And they still have numbers, right?'

'If you say so,' said the man.

'So then I noticed that the room above the pub could be hired out and I said, if we all put in a couple of quid, we could have the place to ourselves once a month, we could talk without being overheard…'

'Why didn't you want to be overheard?' asked the man, suspiciously.

'Oh, only because… well, to people who aren't into it, who don't know that world, it would be meaningless, wouldn't it? All those numbers! And you need to be able to concentrate when you're comparing notes. We like solitude.'

Now the man reached into his file and took out a small notebook with a distinctive red cover. Cam recognised it instantly, saw his own odd little doodles on the cover and a title in his scruffy scrawl: CAM'S NUMBERS.

'Where did you get that?' he gasped.

'From your home.'

Cam glared at him. 'You… went to my home? When?'

'Earlier today. I didn't go. We have uniforms for that.'

'Yes, but why?'

'To get the numbers,' said the man tonelessly.

Cam felt violated by this act. He could feel a wave of resentment building within him but tried to keep it under control. He'd heard too many stories about cops and their rough treatment of suspects. He wiped an arm across his dripping forehead. 'I hope you didn't trash the place,' he said, trying to sound calm. 'I hope you didn't break in. If you'd asked me, I could have got the numbers for you.'

'And you'd have had time to destroy them.'

'Why would I want to do that?' cried Cam. 'There's nothing clandestine about them. I write them down so I can...'

'Yes?' asked the man, as though interested. 'What do you do with them?'

'I...' Cam thought about it and realised with a dull sense of shock, that he didn't actually have a convincing answer. 'I... well ...'

'What do you use them for?' prompted the man.

'I wonder if I might have a glass of water,' said Cam. 'I'm feeling rather...'

'Later! I'll ask again. What are they for?'

'They aren't for anything!'

'Oh, come on.'

'No, honestly! Me and my mates, we... compare them, see which ones are duplicated. We find out where the trains are going, how long they've been in service. Each engine has a name, of course, and we research that.' He thought for a moment. 'The Flying Scotsman! You've heard of it right? It's famous! But why is it called that? Hmm?'

If the man had any idea, he didn't say.

'Because of the speed with which it got from Edinburgh to London back in the nineteen forties! The idea is to get as many names and numbers as you can. Sometimes we go away on short trips to different places, so we can find new trains, new numbers. And we spend time together doing it. We enjoy it. That's not illegal, is it?'

Now the man opened the notebook and indicated a double spread of numbers with dates alongside them. Cam saw that some of them had been circled – not by him – in a different colour. Again, he felt outraged. How dare somebody mess around with his stuff? The man pointed to one number and date which were both circled in bright red.

'What if I told you that our First Minister was riding on that train? On his way to a very important climate change conference. What would you say to that?'

Cam stared at the page for a moment and then made a poor attempt at levity. 'I'd said whoop de doo!' he replied. He glared at the man. 'Coincidence.'

The man indicated another encircled number. 'And this one,' he said. 'The Minister for Education. On his way to London. There was an incident at that meeting. Somebody pulled a gun, tried to shoot him.' He waved a hand at the book. 'There are other "coincidences" in here, far too many for me to list. Suffice to say these are important people going about their work, unaware that they are being spied on.'

'They're not being spied on!' protested Cam. 'Not by me, anyway!'

'So you're doing it on behalf of someone else?'

'No. This is ridiculous!'

'But you are keeping tabs on people's movements?'

'No! I'm really not.' Cam thought for a moment. He licked his lips. His throat felt parched. 'Look, I think I need to talk to a solicitor.'

The man's eyes burned into Cam's. 'I thought you said you were innocent.'

'I am! But… you seem determined to make me look suspicious.'

'You're doing a pretty good job of that on your own,' observed the man. 'You have pages and pages of dates and numbers, several relating to people of national importance. You insist you had no intention of recording their movements. So how else do you explain it?'

'I can't,' protested Cam. 'There's nothing to explain. People ride on trains, that's what they're for isn't it? And there's more of them than ever now when you can't fill a car's fuel tank without taking out a bloody bank loan. And even so, the roads are still gridlocked!'

'So you'd describe yourself as a climate activist, then?'

'No, I bloody wouldn't!' Cam looked helplessly around the room. 'Can't somebody open a window in here?' he pleaded. 'I'm roasting!'

'What do you do with the numbers?' asked the man again, big fat drops of sweat trickling down his own pale features. 'Tell me.'

'I don't do anything with them! I collect them, that's all. Sometimes I look at them. Is that a criminal offence now?' Cam could feel his anger mounting. His clothes were soaked through, and he needed to be out of here. 'Look,' he snarled, 'I have something to say.'

The man seemed amused. 'Do you indeed?' he asked.

'I do. Since I arrived, I've noticed irregularities.'

'Is that right?'

'Yes. I wasn't checked in… and shouldn't this session be recorded or something? You just come waltzing in here like I'm Public Enemy Number One, like I'm something that's stuck to the sole of your shoe. Now you've cooked up this ridiculous theory about train numbers. If you want to know the truth, it sounds like the ramblings of a madman!'

'Have you finished?' asked the man.

'Not quite. I want to talk to your superiors. I want you to fetch somebody who can explain what the hell is going on here. And I want the services of a solicitor. Is that clear?'

There was a short silence in which Cam imagined he could hear the echoes of his final words fading away. The first man shrugged his shoulders, as though it was all out of his hands now. He slid the notebook back into the file and got up from his seat. He turned to look at the second man.

'Explain things to Mr Mcready,' he said and went out of the room.

Cam had quite forgotten about the second man, who was appraising him now with an expression of extreme disappointment.

'Oh dear,' he said. 'Not good.' He uncrossed his arms and walked the short distance to the table. 'You're saying you're not happy with your treatment, is that it?'

The man's voice, like his demeanour, was placid, relaxed.

'All I'm saying,' muttered Cam, 'is that this should have been done by the book. I don't want to make a fuss, but—'

The second man lifted an index finger to his lips and Cam stopped talking abruptly. He noticed that the man's knuckles looked red and raw, as though they'd recently been injured. Cam opened his mouth to say something, but the big man reached out and took him by the shoulders, lifting him gently into an upright position.

'Allow me to explain,' he said.

He smiled sweetly and then punched Cam hard in the stomach, driving all the air out of him and making him double over with a gasp of exhaled breath. Pain spasmed through his body, radiating outward from the place where he had been punched to claim every inch of him. Cam wanted to scream but couldn't catch his breath enough to release it. All that emerged was a ragged groan. The man lowered him into the seat. He stood looking down at Cam for a moment, as though regretting what he had just done – but then he reached out a huge hand to the back of Cam's head and slammed it, face down, onto the table.

Cam was only dimly aware of his nose breaking beneath the impact and then his fevered head filled with flickering explosions of light, from which lumbered the image of a steam train, thick grey smoke pulsing up from its funnel and filling the sky. Cam stayed bent over the table until his breath was back under control and his vision gradually began to clear. He slumped against the back of his chair with a soft moan. He was vaguely surprised to see that the second man had already returned to his place by the wall and that his hands were once again crossed over his chest. He was smiling pleasantly at Cam, the blue eyes vacant, almost innocent, as if the two of them were sharing a joke.

The door opened and the first man came in, the file tucked under one arm, spare hand clutching a couple of paper tissues. He returned to his seat and handed the tissues to Cam, who took them and held them against

PHILIP CAVENEY

the gushing broken thing that was his nose. The action sent fresh pain pulsing across his face. Tears spilled down his cheeks, mingling with the film of acrid sweat. The man opened the file and took out the notebook again. He cleared his throat.

'Here's how we'll do this,' he said, briskly. 'The gatherings will cease with immediate effect. We shall notify the landlord. You will not be drinking in the Outhouse again, you or your friends. You will all be barred.'

'Oh, but—'

The man held up a hand to silence him.

'You shall of course be allowed to frequent other pubs, but there will be no more gatherings, no more booked rooms. And on no account will you meet up with the other three men on that list. Is that clear?'

His friends, his oldest friends…

Cam tried to speak but all that emerged was a formless grunt.

'I shall keep the notebooks and you and your… acquaintances will desist from collecting any more numbers. You will not visit stations or railway lines in Edinburgh or anywhere else. You will find other ways to occupy your time. We will have eyes on you. Do I make myself clear?'

'I don't understand… what if I need to travel somewhere?'

'You will apply to these offices in writing, and we'll see if it can be allowed. Furthermore, before you leave you will sign this form.' The man slid a sheet of paper across the table to Cam, taking care to avoid the splatters of blood on the scarred white surface. He placed a ballpoint pen carefully beside it.

'What does it say?' muttered Cam, his voice muffled by the wadded tissue. He tried to study the words printed on the white page, but his eyes were out of focus and the print was just a blur.

'It's a disclaimer,' said the man, as though that explained everything.

Cam managed a sort of contemptuous snort. 'You'll never get the others to agree,' he said.

'Already signed,' said the man, 'It took some persuading but they complied.'

Cam thought about the state of the big man's knuckles earlier and began to understand.

'We left you till last,' said the man, 'seeing as you were the ringleader.'

'How do you make that out?'

'That's how your friends describe you,' said the man. 'They agreed it was all your idea, that you were the one who was most keen to compare the numbers, to write them down in those little books.'

'But...'

The man seemed to soften for a moment. 'You mentioned steam trains,' he said.' I do remember them. I particularly relish the memory of going with my grandfather along the old Settle to Carlisle railway, one Christmas, when I was a boy. There was light snow but not enough to delay us. When we got to the last stop, Santa Claus was waiting in a wooden grotto and he gave me a present, though I can't remember exactly what it was.' He smiled, shook his head. 'A long time ago. Another world.' His expression hardened again. 'Well, it's a busy day, so it would be good if you could sign this now.' He tapped the form, then glanced over his shoulder

at his companion. 'Or perhaps you require a little more…
explanation?'

Cam shook his head and winced at the pain this
caused. He picked up the pen and signed with a shaking hand.

'Excellent.' The man slid the form into the file. He got
to his feet, seeming well satisfied with his day's work.
'Well, that's us done. You're free to go. Do take a moment
to recover yourself. The door will be left unlocked.' He
stood for a moment as though thinking of offering a hand
to shake but thought better of it. Then his eyes widened
as he remembered something. 'A chemistry set!' he said.
'That's what Santa gave me that day. I believe I still have
the box squirrelled away somewhere.'

He shook his head as if delighted by his own memory.
He turned and walked to the door. The second man followed, and it swung shut behind them.

It was very quiet in the room. Cam sat for a few more
minutes, gingerly probing his nose, wondering whether
he should head back to work or go home. Eventually,
he decided on the latter, telling himself that he needed
to assess what damage had been done there. He might
require the services of a locksmith or a glazier.

An image filled his head, a vivid picture of himself and
his three old friends, sitting around a table in the upstairs
room of the Outhouse, notebooks in front of them, sipping at their beers and crying with laughter about some
stupid joke that one of them had made. He knew now
that those days would never return and a powerful sense
of sadness overtook him.

He brought the wad of bloody tissue up to his face and
cried like a child.

Eventually, he managed to get control of himself. He stood up and walked unsteadily out of the room and along the warren of corridors to the main entrance. He asked the burly cop at reception about his phone and was eventually handed the familiar black oblong, but noticed that it now had a diagonal crack across the screen – and when he tapped it, nothing happened. A cursory inspection told him that the memory card had been removed – the card where a backup of those precious numbers had been stored. Cam sighed and slipped the dead phone into his pocket. He tried to think about where his future might lie but ahead of him, he saw nothing but a forbidding tunnel leading into darkness.

He pushed open the exit door and took a deep breath before stepping out into the cruel heat of the afternoon.

Philip Caveney has been a published author since 1977 and has written fiction for readers of all ages, both as himself and under the pseudonym Danny Weston. In 2007, *Sebastian Darke* was published in twenty countries around the world and shortlisted for the Waterstones Children's Book Prize. In 2016, his novel *The Piper* won the Scottish Children's Book Award and, in 2018, *The Haunting of Jessop Rise* was shortlisted for the Scottish Teen Book Award. He has attended the Edinburgh Literary Salon since relocating to the city in 2015.

FAMILY GATHERINGS

Britta Benson

Before cancer declares war on your blood,
we take you out for a day on the beach.
Not the Bahamas, Jamaica, not even Spain,
just Troon, imagine that! Troon!
A picnic basket and a thermos flask.
Sheer stubbornness on a cold day in May.

You can't believe your luck.
The Firth of Clyde your America.
I hear you giggle, giddy with excitement.
'The sea, the sea, the sea!' you rasp
and your smile flutters across oceans.
Wind blows your thinning grey hair
into a dreamy tuft of angel delights.
Sand in your shoes, salt on your coat,
you play hide and seek with the tide.
You win every time, gain grit and spit,
as you beckon the crests to come closer,
then run, run, run, laugh, like a naughty child.
You pick up shells, pebbles, frosted sea glass,
until your pockets burst with remembrance.

We sit, wrapped bud tight in our jackets,
watch, as you touch worlds for safekeeping.
Do you already know how much we'll need
your warm fingerprints on found treasures
from our day on the beach, for future
    reference?

Limpets now rest on my kitchen window sill,
broken mussels, rocks, still echo your smile.

Britta Benson is a circus skills instructing German, writer, performer, and linguist thriving in Scotland, her chosen habitat since the year 2000. She runs a creative writing group, The Procrastinators, and writes a daily blog, 'Britta's Blog – Letters from Scotland', as well as her poetry blog, 'Odds & Ends'.

BONE CHINA

Stuart Johnstone

---

i

'Which way is anti-clockwise?'
     Nan spun a gnarled but pristinely painted finger around the rim of Margaret's teacup. 'This way,' she said, 'but first finish. Just leave a dribble at the bottom.'

The woman opposite sipped nervously.

'Now, just what you can afford, mind,' said Nan handing her a black satin drawstring bag.

'Oh right.' Margaret lowered the cup and forced a swallow before plucking some coins from her purse and dropping them into the bag. Her eyes scanned Nan's front room as she sat quietly, returning to the cup, forcing down the tea she was almost too nervous to drink. Pictures in brass frames were dotted around the walls displaying odd folk in odder garments doing God knows what. She drew another mouthful from the cup and was aghast to see that she was barely halfway done.

'Try to relax, dear. I'm not going to hurt you.' Nan patted Margaret's arm, sending it into a shake that Margaret had to correct with her other hand. Her wedding ring rattled on the rim of the cup as she did.

'Careful, dear; that's my good china,' said Nan before coughing into her sleeve, a heaving, rattling burst. When she'd recovered, she stood and turned off the ceiling light, leaving only the largely insufficient lamp in the centre of the round table to see by.

'Sorry, Nan. I'm just a bit on edge, you know? That's a nasty sounding cough. These summer colds are just the worst aren't they?'

Nan nodded as another short fit of coughing took her. She dabbed at her mouth with a handkerchief as it eased, leaving a purple smudge from her lipstick, the same plum shade as her nails, Margaret saw.

'It… it's lovely crockery, Nan.' Margaret spun the cup in her hand, taking in the intricate design.

'Bone china it is,' Nan said as she sat and composed herself. 'It was my mother's and her mother's before. Do you know why they call it bone china?'

Margaret shook her head. It was all she could do as the latest mouthful flat refused to go down.

'It's made from bone-ash, you see. It's what gives it its strength. Means they can make it really thin and stays nice and sturdy.'

Margaret's cup began to rattle again in its saucer so she carefully laid it down on the table. 'What? Like real bones?'

'Oh yes. Traditionally cattle bones. It has to be bone china for an accurate reading. It's the connection to the dead.' Nan sat forward in her chair, her voice lowered. 'Thing about this set, Margaret, my granny swore blind it was made from no animal bones.' Nan allowed a short silence to fall between them, before sitting back and asking with a brighter tone: 'Are you about done, dear? Shall we get started?'

'Mmm,' gurgled Margaret, swallowing and relieved to see she actually was.

'Three and six, Margaret?' said Nan emptying the contents of the velvet bag onto the table in front of her. Her nose wrinkled as she pushed the coins around the tablecloth.

'Oh, um, I'm sorry, Nan. I wasn't sure what was appropriate and my Michael hasn't been too well of late. Here I might have another shilling.' Margaret frantically raked through her bag for another coin and slid it towards the others.

'Only if you can afford it, dear. It does take its toll, but I wouldn't have you left short. Nan palmed the coins back into the drawstring bag before Margaret had a chance to consider this. 'Now,' Nan continued, 'take the cup handle in your left hand and rotate it like I showed you, three times.'

'Like this?' There was a soft grinding sound as the porcelain rim slid around the basin of the saucer.

'That's it. Now, place your hand on the cup and take a moment to think about what it is you want the leaves to show us.'

Nan placed her own hand atop Margaret's and closed her eyes. She gave a sharp intake of breath and the lamp reacted, buzzing and crackling and fading to almost nothing, sending the room into near darkness before snapping back to full light.

'Oh dear God in heaven,' shrieked Margaret seeing Nan's eyes now open but not as they were. Two lifeless white pools stared back at her. She tried to draw away but Nan held her hand fast and the room went black for a second, drawing another stifled yelp from Margaret.

'Relax, dear,' said Nan as the light returned and with it, Nan's brown eyes. 'Now, turn the cup over, place it on the saucer and push it here.'

Margaret did as she was told, with the cup threatening to shake itself clear of the saucer.

'Let's see what we have then, dear.' Nan applied the spectacles that hung on a chain around her neck and inspected the interior of the cup. 'Hmm, interesting.'

'What do you see, Nan?'

'Well, you see this symbol here, looks like a bishop chess piece?'

'Um, yes; I suppose,' Margaret lied.

'Well, this means significant worry. You've had something chewing away at you it seems?'

'Michael's not been himself, that's what that must be. He gets irritable if I try to talk to him about it. Can you see what it is?'

'Well, the leaves are rarely that specific, Margaret, but let me have a look. Oh, that's interesting?'

Margaret leaned in, but to her, the black smudges at the bottom of the cup were just that.

'You see here,' said Nan thrusting a plum-lacquered pinkie nail inside. 'This church spire; it means a clear way ahead.' Nan looked up to see a confusion wrinkling Margaret's nose. 'Means everything is alright. Some ailment, that for whatever reason he hasn't shared with you, but it's nothing to fret about.'

'Oh really? Well that's a relief, Nan. You've no idea how—'

'Now, this is interesting,' Nan cut in.

'What? What is it?'

'This symbol here, clear as day it is, can you see?'

Margaret squinted into the cup again. 'This one on the left? Sort of looks like a star?'

'Not a star, see this trail coming from it, something like… a stem?'

'Oh it's a flower? Yes, I see it.'

'Very good Margaret, perhaps you have something of the sight yourself.'

Margaret flushed and smiled. 'What does it mean?'

'Well, this is not just any flower, Margaret. It's a peonie, which means a very important decision is looming, and next to this other symbol, that's clearly a weasel; it means it has to do with strangers.'

Margaret sat back in her chair, her eyes searching the ceiling. 'I cannae think.'

'It may not be your decision, maybe someone close to you?'

Margaret's head shook gently. 'No, it doesn't mean anything to—'

'A decision about strangers, very important, might not be you exactly,' said Nan, a little too sharply.

'Oh wait. I wonder if it could be about my Michael? Yes, that might be it. You know that group of travellers camped outside the village?'

'Hmmm, I think maybe I heard something or other.'

'Aye, well there's many want rid of them and the community council are voting as to whether they should evict them off the land, and my Michael's on that council.'

'Oh, is he?'

'Well, he doesn't know quite which way to go. You know, Christian compassion on the one hand and there's the people of the village to—'

'Well, I don't know about all that, Margaret, I'm

not a learned woman. All I can tell you is what I see here.'

'What do you see, Nan?'

'The weasel means nothing but mischief, Margaret. And worse: the weasel is facing a flag here; danger indeed.'

'So, wait…' Margaret leaned across the table once again to look at the symbols, the ones that looked remarkably like random smudges. 'The weasel is my Michael?'

A snort of breath escaped Nan's flared nostrils. 'No, Margaret, the weasel represents the mischief, the… no good element, and if your astute assessment of the reading is correct, in this circumstance that would be?'

Margaret thought on this, her head shaking again. 'The council?'

Nan brought her own teacup to her rouged lips and tried to not to roll her eyes.

'… or maybe the gypsies?'

Margaret jumped and clutched her bag to her chest as Nan's had slapped the table. 'Bingo,' she said. 'Now, what you do with that information is entirely your concern, Margaret. But if you ask me, an insight such as this? Well, there is an obligation attached to it? Wouldn't you say?'

'I, uh. I mean, I suppose. Although it's not really my place to—'

'Well, I'm not going to tell you your place, Margaret,' said Nan, gingerly getting out of her chair and ushering Margaret out of hers. She placed an arm around her shoulder and began leading her down the hall towards the door. 'All I'll say is this: if I were to receive such valuable foresight as this and I failed to do anything with it, well, I'd have to live with a heavy conscience indeed. Wouldn't you say?'

ii

The queue for the post office on a Wednesday would invariably snake clear out of the door and halfway along the street, moving along at glacier pace. The uninitiated might despair and see it as time lost. To a veteran, Wednesdays were a delicious opportunity for the exchange of gossip while you waited to collect your pension.

'It's egg or cheese and pickle.'

'Give us an egg, Celia.'

Celia, or Mrs Mavis – the Doctor's wife as she was better known in the village – peeled back the tinfoil wrap to reveal four crustless triangles. Nan poured two cups from her thermos but had to quickly pass them until her coughing abated.

'Summer colds—'

'Just the worst, I know,' said Nan collecting herself, and then her lunch from Celia.

'Listen, Nan, I feel last week I may have been a trifle indiscreet,' said Celia in a whisper. Out in the street there would have been no need to lower the voice, with a dozen conversations happening in both directions, but now that the queue had shifted inside the building, voices had become more subdued. 'You will keep what I told you about Margaret's husband to yourself won't you?'

'Of course, Celia, you know anything you say to me is taken to the grave,' said Nan.

The queue shifted forward and the ladies slid their mobile picnic along the shelf beside them, ordinarily utilised for the filling-in of forms, or addressing of envelopes.

'I mean, though, it's a sin keeping that sort of thing

from your own wife, embarrassing though it may be. There ought not to be any secrets between a man and his wife, do you not agree?' Celia again checked they were not being overheard, pretending she was adjusting the scarf housing her hair-rollers.

'Mmm-hmm,' nodded Nan, her mouth full of egg.

'Like a bunch of grapes, John said; never seen a case of haemorrhoids like it,' said Celia, lowering her voice now lower again. 'Still, it's not something you should keep to yourself. Not like Mrs McTear's boy; an aggressive dose of gonorrhoea apparently. Now that's the kind of thing you tell nobody.'

'Nan, Mrs Mavis,' said Danny Wilson sheepishly, trying not to disturb the ladies', clearly private, conversation as he made his way out.

'Danny, son, how are you? You keepin'… well?'

Danny allowed Nan a second to compose herself as she coughed furiously into a tissue. 'Aye, no bad thanks, Nan. Best I can at least. You're okay?' Danny's brow furrowed and was about to place a hand on the old lady's shoulder before she straightened herself and cleared her throat.

'I'm fine, son. Just one of those summer things. So, you're still havin' no luck finding a job, dear? Never mind, you keep at it. I see nothing but good things in your future.'

'Aw, well if you say it, Nan, then I believe it, thanks,' said Danny waving goodbye with his benefit book.

'Work-shy that laddie,' said Nan, back into a whisper. 'Times might be hard but you're no out of work a full year unless you're trying to avoid it, if you ask me.'

'People living on hand-outs, a disgrace,' said Celia pointing her sandwich at the door, but then began wrapping it back into foil as she was ushered forward to a desk.

It had been bright and sunny for almost two weeks straight, perhaps approaching some kind of record, but all that was coming to an end. You didn't need to be the village mystic to see the thick rolling grey in the distant sky was a sure sign that things were on the change.

On Nan's suggestion the ladies returned not by Main Street, but by the Old Mill path, taking them down by the river and the field adjacent to the McAndrew farm on the edge of the village by the roadway.

'Would you look, still there,' said Celia. She gestured out at the circle of tents, horses and wagons and domed, wooden caravans.

Nan tutted and shook her head. 'I thought this was all… sorted. The council voted didn't they?'

'They did,' confirmed Celia.

Their path drew them closer. Nan could see that the rear of one of the horse-drawn caravans was lowered towards the road, there appeared to be items for sale, arranged in a row across the polished wooden flap.

'Well after our talk last week I felt I had to say something to John. "It's council business" says he, but I explained to him, it's the business of the whole village thank you very much and he needn't take that kind of superior tone with me, I'm not one of his patients,' said Celia.

'Mmm-hmm.'

As they approached, it became clear that the travellers were packing up. Here and there men were pulling boxes onto the carts.

'I feel sorry for the next town they pitch up their rickety old caravans in, of course, but we have to look after ourselves, don't we?' said Celia.

'Of course. I mean, Christian charity is all fine and well, until they steal the lead from the church roof.' Nan whispered the last few words as a dark-haired woman appeared at the hatch of the caravan.

'Afternoon ladies. Might I interest you in a keepsake?'

The woman was very pretty, Nan could not deny her that, with her wavy dark locks, olive skin, and rouged lips, but she was likely as filthy as a stray dog in that mobile hut of hers, she decided.

'What are these things?' Nan said, picking up a ragged piece of pink glass made into some kind of necklace by a leather thong wrapped around it.

'That one is a rose crystal. It will bring calmness and fruitfulness to your marriage.'

The woman's accent was thick, maybe too thick, Nan considered. What better way to sell worthless tack than making it seem… exotic. 'Mmm-hmm.' Nan raised the thing and let it spin on its cord. 'Even if my Basil hadn't passed, five years back, I very much doubt a pink rock would bring calmness to that cantankerous sod,' she said to Celia out the corner of her mouth, though not at all quietly.

Celia chuckled and plucked another item from the assortment. 'And what do you call this?' she said, squinting at the furry thing in her hand.'

'A charm, for luck,' said the seller.

'Put that down, Celia. It's probably crawling with fleas, or worse.'

Celia quickly dropped it amongst the other items.

'It's a rabbit's foot, Celia. As worthless as all this junk.' Nan waved the back of her hand across the other pendants, necklaces, and whatnots.

'It's true to say that we bring our own luck and blessings to these charms, and in that respect they carry value to the bearer. But I see these are not for you. Instead, I will read your palm. Please come.'

Nan was horrified to see Celia was reaching out to take the hand of the filthy woman who stretched down over the trinkets. Nan slapped Celia away.

'You'll do no such thing, Celia. Palm reading indeed. You might as well throw your money in a ditch. If it's a reading you want, you come to me.' Nan was about to enter into a rant about this charlatan who would surely have a crystal ball tucked back there, maybe those devil worshiping picture cards too, but a movement in the back of the caravan had caught her attention. A painfully thin thing darted away as soon as she had been seen. 'Come on, Celia,' she said instead and pulled the doctor's wife away from the hatch.

iii

Nan woke with a start in her armchair, sending the book on her lap to the floor. She remained still for a moment trying to decide if she'd dreamt the knock at the door that had woken her; but then it came again, three slow thuds.

The girl on the doorstep looked as if gravity bore her a grudge, that it affected her more severely than everyone else. Her long dark hair clung to the sides of her face as the rain pounded on the world outside. The jacket she wore, an old green canvas thing, hung like a sheet on a twig. It looked to be a man's jacket with the rolled-up sleeves still draped beyond her hands.

'Can I help you?' said Nan, looking past and around the girl for an accompanying adult, but there was none.

'You're the lady who does readings,' said the girl, a statement, not a question Nan noted.

'That's right, but only usually for friends and such. I don't think I know you, do I, lassie?'

'Please,' the girl said. 'I have money.' The girl reached into the seemingly cavernous pockets of the coat and produced a handful of coins.

Nan was about to send her on her way but spotted a few silver amongst the copper. 'Hmm,' she breathed, causing her to cough into the back of her hand. She cleared her throat and said: 'It'll be the quick version. And don't sit on anything 'til you're dry.'

The girl's face lit up lit and she slipped past Nan into the house. Nan grabbed a towel, a used one, from the linen basket, and went after her.

'Dry yourself off while I make the tea, and leave that jacket by the door, you're dripping on the rug.'

Nan removed the coat from the slip of a girl; no older than twelve she assessed, squeezing at her hair with the towel.

She inspected the girl and, considering her dry enough, told her to sit at the table. She poured two cups and slid one across to the girl who was rubbing and breathing on her hands.

'That'll warm you; now drink your tea up.' Nan took up her own cup and drank greedily by way of example. 'Where did you come from?' she asked.

'Oh, lots of places, and nowhere particularly.'

Nan considered this answer a moment. 'You're one of them travellers, aren't you?'

'That's right, Romany.'

Ha, Romany, Nan thought. Roamin' and thieving, more like. Roamin' and contributing nothing. 'That's no life for a girl your age.'

'I dunno,' said the girl. 'Guess I don't know any other way, but I get to see lots of places and I've lots of friends—'

'Education, stability,' Nan cut in.

'What?'

Nan sighed and thought better of pursuing. 'Are you about done?'

'Nearly. It tastes yucky. I can only sip it.'

'Well, keep sipping. And here, pop your money in this.' Nan tossed the velvet bag across the table.

The girl put down her cup and began struggling with the drawstring. She made to drop the money in but fumbled and coins rolled across the table in all directions with a few chinking to the floor. Nan tutted as she took the bag with a swipe and went searching the floor.

'Sorry, my hands are cold from the rain,' the girl said, but didn't really look sorry, as far as Nan was concerned.

In her frustration, Nan almost forgot the routine but she took a deep breath, feeling the weight of the bag with some satisfaction. 'Do you like the cup?' she said, getting back on track.

The girl held hers up, inspecting the Chinese pattern, and shrugged. 'I guess so.'

'Bone China it is. Do you know why they call it—'

'Who are all these people?' The girl was looking around at the pictures up on the walls.

'Mystics from around the world.'

'They're friends of yours?'

'No, not friends as such.'

'We have pictures at home, but only of people we actually know.'

Home, Nan thought. 'Are you finished?'

'Uhu.'

'Good, now turn the cup over and twist anticlockwise in the saucer three times… No, the other way. Now, turn the cup back up and pass it over.'

'Wait, you're going too fast.'

'That's good enough,' said Nan who stood and pulled the cup towards her. 'Right let's have a look. Oh wait,' said Nan, her hand hovering above the cup. 'What is it you want to know?'

'Oh, um, Mama's not been too well; I want to know when she's going to get better.'

'Alright,' said Nan. She closed her eyes and held her hand flat, an inch or so above the cup. She pushed the heel of her foot into the lump in the rug under the table where the lamp wire was loose, causing it to buzz and dim. She took a few deep breaths and opened her eyes again, the whites staring out at the girl. She was distracted by a chuckle. Nan's eyes spun brown again and she lifted her foot from the rug. The girl, mouth agape like a goldfish snatched from its bowl, was trying to force her eyes to the back of her head, but the deep green of her irises were still clearly visible under her stretched lids.

'What are you doing?'

'Have you always been able to do that with your eyes? Am I doing it? Am I?'

'Cut that out,' Nan barked. 'This isn't a joke.'

The girl stopped chuckling and folded her arms. Nan pushed her glasses on. The girl's legs swung irritably, not quite long enough to reach the floor.

'Right, where was I?' Nan said with an exasperated breath. 'Let's just see what we've got.' Nan leaned the cup into the light of the lamp.

She was silent for a full minute.

'Is something wrong?' asked the girl.

'What? Ah, no… not wrong, it's just…'

'What?'

'Well, it's rarely this clear.' Nan stared at the symbols which had formed more perfectly than if she'd taken paint and brush to the cup. 'The owl and the bat together,' she said. Like they were dancing, Nan thought. 'I'm sorry, lassie, your mother's sick, very sick, and death is coming for her soon. I'm… I'm sorry, lassie.'

'Interesting,' said the girl, showing remarkable complacency in the face of such news.

'What do you mean, "interesting"?' Nan removed her glasses. The girl wore a peculiar expression.

The visitor stood and collected her coat. 'Mama thought you were an old fraud; thought you might need teaching a bit of a lesson. Turns out you have the sight after all,' she said, with a maturity that unsettled Nan. 'Besides, seems like you have enough to worry about.'

'What? What are you talking about, lassie? Go on with you. Get you out of my house.'

Nan heard the girl unlatching the door, but she was busy looking at the cup in her hand, the cup she'd been reading. That's when she noticed a plum smear at the rim. She opened her mouth to talk, what kind of trick?

But a coughing fit took her. She rasped into her sleeve and thought about the coins she'd plucked from the floor.

'Out, get out,' she wheezed.

'Them summer colds,' said the girl, opening the door, 'they're just the worst.'

Stuart Johnstone was selected as an 'emerging Edinburgh writer' by the forerunners of the Edinburgh Literary Salon, UNESCO City of Literature Trust in 2015. Since then, he's gone on to publishing success as a crime novelist. His third novel *Run to Ground* was published in November 2022. Stuart lives and works in Edinburgh and has remained a proud friend of the Edinburgh Literary Salon.

HAEMATOLOGY DAY UNIT

Kirsty MacDonald

I tick tock with the rest of them,
swaying and upright,
my best impression of calm.
We are the hands that clasp
and unclasp.
We are the swapping,
numb legs, desperately casual.
We are the occasional wrist check
that ignores the clock on the wall.
All in our usual seats,
pretending we're not listening
to the doctor's apology, to the lottery,
to the numbers on his sheet.
The lower your count,
the longer you stay.
All of us together, three times a week,
pretending we don't know each other's
     surnames.
Pretending we don't notice when someone –
anyone –
stops coming back.

Kirsty MacDonald is a writer living in West Lothian. As a graduate of the University of Dundee's MLitt Creative Writing programme, Kirsty has had her work published online and in an anthology of British Poets, *A Bee's Breakfast*, in 2017. She is currently creating work alongside the Calder Development Trust heritage project

LAVENDER AND DEATH

Mark Lewis

L ucy didn't think anything was wrong when she saw the first Plague Doctor as she was walking her son, George, to school. It was normal to see people dressed strangely in Edinburgh, but Lucy felt that a full costume complete with leather hat, goggles, beak, long leather coat, and boots at 8:30 in the morning was unreasonable. It looked too expensive and unnerving to be a stag or hen costume and the person wearing it was almost freakishly tall in Lucy's view. Their arms and legs looked longer than she would have expected. There was something that looked unsettling about them, beyond the strange attire.

Lucy reasoned that it could just be a lost extra from a spooky Scotland tour or perhaps someone on the way to rehearse for a Fringe show, although it wasn't the season. Maybe they would break into a TikTok dance routine at any moment. Frankly, so close in time to a lockdown caused by a pandemic, she felt that the costume was in bad taste.

George grasped Lucy's hand tighter, which was not like him.

'I don't like it, Mum,' he said.

'It's okay,' said Lucy. She spoke close to him so no one else would hear. 'It's just someone dressed up.'

'No,' George said. 'He doesn't look right and it's too dark around him.'

'It's Edinburgh in autumn, of course it's dark, George.'

'No. Just around him. He's not supposed to be here.'

Lucy felt a chill beyond what the touch of the cold air would bring. George was right. There was a darkness around the Plague Doctor deeper than shadow. An un natural gloom gathered around him.

Things felt more normal once Lucy had dropped George off at the school. Most of the parents still wore masks. It was good to at least see other people but she was not used to it yet and felt on edge. She made brief, polite acknowledgements to a couple of parents she recognised before walking home. She tried to put the Plague Doctor out of her mind, told herself she had just lost perspective.

Her heart beat too fast as she walked, feeling that she was being followed. Walking down the leafy main road, she was sure she could see a dark leathery form out of the corner of her eye, but when she turned and looked there was nothing out of the ordinary. Just a morning dog walker. As she reached the courtyard car park in her block of flats, Lucy looked at Brian's empty parking space. She wished he was still working from home. It had been irritating having him there but she missed him now and his company would have been reassuring. She realised her hand was shaking as she put the key in the front door.

Even working from home Lucy needed some routine, so she put her coffee machine on, fired up her laptop, and found some music to play on her phone. Work felt somehow grounding, dull as it was, largely involving reconciling figures on spreadsheets. For all the stress and the demands of her clients, she had been busy through the lockdowns and the work had helped her through. Typing away, Lucy's day became reassuringly mundane and she put the strangeness of the morning out of her mind until her first coffee break. It was then, sipping her coffee, looking out of the window into the car park, that she saw them. Lucy felt a quick pang of shock. There were three of them. Three Plague Doctors, of differing shapes and sizes. Again, each of them looked wrong, out of kilter with the reality around them. They did not appear to talk or noticeably communicate with each other. Darkness pooled around them. Lucy reasoned that they hadn't actually done anything overtly bad enough to justify her calling the police, especially since they had recently lifted the restrictions on how many people could gather in one place outdoors.

She decided to take pictures. She could send them to Brian in a jokey tone but seeking reassurance, 'Is it just me or are these guys creepy?'. Or, on second thoughts, she could ask for advice on Facebook, as she didn't want Brian to think she was losing it from being at home on her own too much. Perhaps there was a strange Plague Doctor-related event in Edinburgh.

She looked at them through her phone but a strange pixelation blocked them out so she couldn't get a clear picture. Her heart beat faster. She looked through her phone at her room, then switched it to reverse to look at herself, then back at the Plague Doctors. The pixelation only happened when she looked at the Plague Doctors through her phone. It was impossible to get a picture of them. She googled 'Plague Doctors' and 'Edinburgh'. There were some articles about a prank in May 2020 and some articles relating to the bubonic plague, but nothing current.

Lucy finished her work, focusing as best she could through her anxiety, glancing out of the window constantly in case they should come closer to her block's front door. They did not move, but neither did they leave. The usual vans came and went for deliveries and property maintenance. Work dragged and she knew she would have to go through everything again when she was feeling less agitated.

As usual, her neighbour Craig went out for a smoke in the car park. Should she warn him? she wondered. Was there anything to really warn him of? With a morbid curiosity she felt guilty for, she watched him. As he rolled up, he did not appear to acknowledge that the Plague Doctors were there. But he avoided the area they were occupying, despite it being his usual spot to smoke in.

Lucy rushed through lunch time and bathroom breaks as she could not tear herself away from her seat by the window for long, in case those *things* came closer. A banging at the door shattered her concentration. Nerves on edge, she jumped at the sound, then still shaking, walked to the door as quietly as she could and looked through the spyhole. No one was there. She composed herself. It was probably just an Amazon delivery. She couldn't remember ordering anything but maybe Brian had and hadn't mentioned it. Lucy put the chain on the door, opened it and looked out. No one appeared to be around. There was a large box outside her door. There was no name or address on it, but she took it in.

Lucy brought the box into the kitchen and opened it with a pair of scissors. The contents smelled of leather and lavender. She recoiled when she saw what was inside. Two Plague Doctor costumes, one her size, one child-sized. It would fit George. Was this some kind of sick prank? She closed the box and put it in one of the few empty floor spaces in the cramped flat.

Returning to work, Lucy stared at her laptop but her attention was light. The numbers just weren't reconciling while her mind was racing. She would have to go over the figures again once George was back. She could not help but keep glancing out of the window to check if *they* were still there and in case they came closer, even though keeping watch would not affect the situation. At last, the time came to pick George up from school, there was no way to avoid the confrontation. No back exits from the block of flats. Past the Plague Doctors was the only way to leave the block. They were still gathered in the car park, but there were five now.

She found it difficult enough to leave the flat at the best of times now. The lockdown had brought a fear of the outdoors and of a plague that could be caught by touching a bin, breathing in too close to someone, shaking hands. With those things out there, it was near to impossible to go outside. Only the thought of George drove her from the safety of the flat. She had to pick him up from school, despite whoever or whatever those things were. For a moment she considered putting on the Plague Doctor suit that had been delivered earlier, but no, that felt wrong.

Lucy left it as long as she could without risking being late. She took a deep breath and summoned from somewhere the strength to stand up, put her leather jacket on, and approach the door. She opened it. The corridor was quiet. Her heart pounded as she pushed the block's front door. It swung open hard and Lucy rushed out, braced for something terrible. She held the door open with her foot as she scanned the car park. They were gone. Then, footsteps in the corridor behind her – she gasped and turned around. Immediately she felt like a fool, it was just Craig, with his bag of roll-ups and tobacco.

'Alright?' Craig asked.

She nodded, too flustered to answer directly. Then, recovering herself, 'Yes. Stressful day.'

'Same,' Craig said, skinning up his tobacco. Lucy looked at the roll-up, maybe she needed an addiction like that to calm her nerves. She contemplated asking Craig about the Plague Doctors – had he seen them? But she did not want him to think she was crazy.

Lucy left the car park without further incident and hurried to the school, through the streets with their imposing Georgian Bath stone buildings. She tried to focus just on where she was going. The roads were noisy with cars, the streets as busy as normal at this time of day. Then she saw them, dotted around in small groups. More Plague Doctors. Lucy chose to ignore them, she noted where they were so she could avoid them but did not look directly at them. She knew without looking that they still appeared somehow out of kilter with the reality around them.

As Lucy approached the school, she saw with horror that the gates were surrounded by Plague Doctors and the area in front of the gates was consumed by darkness. The only way she could reach the entrance to meet George was by joining the throng. She had to do it for George. As she joined the crowd, she could smell lavender first, then leather, but underneath that there was a reek of death. No one talked, but as *it* turned to her, it made a wet clicking noise. In the midst of these things, she could no longer see the sky. The darkness enveloped her. She clenched her shaking hand and fought through to the front. It was like wading through thick water. Reaching the gates, she could see the slate grey sky again and school yard.

With relief, Lucy saw that the children and teachers emerged from the school buildings with the usual excitement and there were no Plague Doctors among them. George came out waving a piece of paper with a painting of a tree on it. She hugged him too tightly, so he pulled a face. Looking around now, the Plague Doctors had gone, replaced by masked parents. There were none she knew well, only a couple she recognised vaguely by sight. They gave her strange looks and kept their distance.

On the way home, George regaled her with how they had gone to the nearby park to gather inspiration. She felt a chill when she saw the deep-black painted Plague Doctor looking around the tree trunk.

'Was that there?' Lucy said pointing at it.

George shrugged. 'I liked drawing it. Are you okay, Mum?'

'I'm just stressed.'

'You don't need to be scared,' said George.

'Of what?'

'Everything changes.'

Lucy didn't press him for more information, but instead focused on getting them home. Avoiding getting too close to any of the Plague Doctors who had assembled on the corners of streets, at the park's gates… they were everywhere now. All shapes and sizes. Parent and child Plague Doctors walking home, a bus full of Plague Doctors in the static traffic, Plague Doctors in cars, in vans. Plague Doctors in shops, lining the streets, and everywhere around them was darkness.

Heart beating fast, she grasped George's hand tightly and tried to walk purposefully, ignoring the thickening groups of Plague Doctors.

Two Plague Doctors stood at the entry to the car park in front of the block of flats then, inside the car park, more formed a corridor, like a gauntlet of warriors in an initiation. They stood still as Lucy passed through them, grasping George's hand tightly, hurrying. She could not help but notice that smell again, and those wet clicking noises.

Lucy felt a rush of hope when she saw Brian's familiar Audi in its parking space. Whatever was going on, Brian would make it okay. She didn't stop walking until they were back in the flat, where she slammed and locked the door behind them. She leaned against the door, out of breath.

'It's time, Mum,' George said.

'What?'

'Daddy's home. It's time for change.'

George slipped his hand out of Lucy's and ran to the living room where Brian stood, fully dressed in a Plague Doctor uniform. She recognised it was him by the way he stood, by the eyes she could see through the goggles. The box with the Plague Doctor costumes was there, in front of Brian. George ran forward and collected his from the box, and eagerly started putting on the beak and goggles while making strange clicking noises. Brian picked up the other costume and started walking towards her. Part of her wanted to run and not look back. She looked at George putting on his mask and knew she had no choice. She took a deep breath and held out her steady hand.

Mark Lewis is Edinburgh-based and attends the Edinburgh Literary Salon. He has had over twenty-five short stories and several poems published, and three panto-mimes performed. He performs his poems and stories throughout Edinburgh and was a runner up in the Leith Festival Story Slam. His latest work is a solo journalling role-playing game about Greek gods, goddesses, champions and monsters, as part of the Edinburgh Indie Gamers zine which is currently funding on Kickstarter.

ANTEBELLUM

Marcas Mac an Tuairneir

an dlùth-phàirteachas le muinntir na h-Ùcraine

Bidh an saoghal, air bliadhna sam bith,
a' tilleadh dhan aon àite
    mar gun dèan e laighe
air ais   ann an leabaidh dual nan tìm,
gathan grèine nan ruith, uair eile,
thar làraich ciùrraidh,
slocan nach deach fhàgail
le mì-chliath chaoran,
ag itealaich o chian ciar nan cian
de dhomhan gun chnuasadh

Ach, 's iad a shoilleiricheas
faoineachas a' chinne-daonna,
a' tar-dhìreadh crìochan mas fhìor,
do-fhaicsinneach bho ar gealaich mhaslaichte.

In solidarity with the people of Ukraine

The world, on any given year,
returns to the same place
      as if it slots
back   into the tessellation of the times,
the sun's rays, running, once more
over sites of trauma,
craters left not
in the wake of freak conjunction with meteors,
winging their way from the outmost depths
of a universe, we cannot contemplate.

Instead, they illuminate
our human folly, transcending
even the imagined borders, invisible,
from the vantage of our mortified moon.

Tha gach mòr-chùis air a bàthadh
le suail an làin fholcanaich fhalcanaich,
sàr-ghorm anns a' ghuirmean agus deachdairean
ri onfhadh ris an aigeann,
an dùirn air am bùird màrmoir ughaich
bhon stùir iad stàitean,   gam mùchadh
am measg ceòl nan co-chruinnean.

Leis gach cuairt, èirigh Eòrpa
bho dhuibhre na oidhche,   ga tòn-bhreith
de phit dhubh Thalheim:
tha na rionnagan
air seo fhaicinn
roimhe.

The grandiose is drowned,
by the swell of the tide, swirling
ultramarine in the indigo and dictators
raging into the abyss,
their fists on the marble ellipses
of their tables of state   tuned-out
amidst the music of spheres.

With each orbit, Europe emerges
from the obscurity of night,   breech-born
of the pit of Talheim:
The stars have
seen all this
before.

Marcas Mac an Tuairneir is a poet and singer-songwriter, based in Edinburgh. He is the author of four collections. The latest *Polaris* (2022) was shortlisted for the Saltire Scottish Poetry Book of the Year Award and a Saboteur Award. He was the winner of the Wigtown Gaelic Poetry Competition in 2017, having been shortlisted on four occasions. His third collection, *Dùileach* (2020), was shortlisted for the Derick Thomson Prize. His debut album *Speactram* (2022) saw him shortlisted as Gaelic Singer of the Year at the MG ALBA Scots Trad Music Awards.

BY THE LIGHT OF BRÌGHDE

Charlie Roy

Shrina scraped her hair back into her bonnet. They were going to be late again. No matter how long she allowed for them to find their jumpers, put their shoes on, and pull on their coats, it always took longer.

'Thighearna, glèidh mi![1] Where's your boot, Àdhamh? No, you did not come back from a' bhun-sgoil[2] in just one.'

She turned to call up the stairs.

'A Chailein, a Shorcha, we need to go, greasaibh oirbh![3] We'll be late again!'

She pulled her phone out of her coat pocket to check the time. 18:43. Of course, if it were just her, she could be in the square with five minutes to spare at a brisk pace, but the weans move so slow. Maybe the Bains's would be just ahead. At least the kids would dash to catch them, and she wouldn't have to listen to the whole chat about Minecraft Alba's online fire festivals. No matter what

---

[1] Thighearna, glèidh mi! – Lord, save me!
[2] a' bhun-sgoil – primary school
[3] greasaibh oirbh! – hurry up

the kids might say, it was so much better to attend in person. The White Dancers looked so lovely backlit by the fire.

Her husband and daughter had finally come down. At least they both looked properly dressed. Cailean usually wore sportswear, as though he would suddenly need to leap into a quick game of iomain[4] or bàl-coise[5]. Today, he had his kilt on – with a jumper, it wasn't a formal occasion after all. They pulled their outdoor layers on and started out of the door. Shrina threw a Dentastix to Nessie, their black lab.

'Back soon, a nighean bheag.[6]'

She checked the time again. 18:49. It would be a rush, but they'd get there. Taing do shealbh.[7] Shrina considered giving them the talk about Creutairean Draoidheil.[8] Surely they knew well enough by now. Though only a few weeks ago that poor lady in Kirksheen almost lost her wee boy to the faeries. It was all over the village Facebook. Another woman had disappeared at the same time, but that might have been unconnected. Who knew, it might simply have been clickbait. She'd read all the comments on the post. Wild speculation and dour shutdowns. Nonetheless, ever since the Gaelic had come back into everyday use in the Republic of Alba, the magic beasties had come back. Why else would there be an entire specialist police department, the Supernatural Division.

---

[4] iomain – shinty
[5] bàl-coise – football
[6] a nighean bheag – little girl
[7] Taing do shealbh – thank goodness
[8] Creutairean draoidheil – magical creatures

Words have power, no doubting it. Unless it was when trying to get your own weans to do anything.

She smiled to herself and caught Cailean's eye. He looked happy. The brisk pace up the wee hill behind the house, before the gentle walk down to the heart of the village, had brought the colour to his cheeks, and his eyes sparkled. The frustration of trying to get out of the door evaporated. It was a lovely clear night, they were together, and the Quarter Day Fire festivals were always good fun. They'd met at a fire festival – Beltane, back when it was on Calton Hill in Edinburgh. Hard to believe this was still the same world. Back then it was just an Instagram-able event to tick off your #YOLO list and hashtag with wee slogans like #ScotlandForever and some bad Gaelic.

They reached the village square. Àdhamh and Sorcha had already spotted their school friends and were tugging at Shrina's coat to be allowed to go. She scanned the crowd, already knowing that she was going to let them go. It would be safe enough.

'A chlann, èistibh.[9] You stay in the square. You don't go to your friends' houses. No, not even Kemi's. After the dance, come back to find us, we'll be near this big tree, and I'll get you a warm milk each. Yes, and some sweets. Have fun.'

They scampered off. Shrina rubbed her eight-arm cross amulet. It was the first gift Cailean had given her. It had the face of the Goddess Kali in the middle, a perfect combination for her. She often wondered why the Hindu creatures hadn't reappeared like so many others,

---

[9] A chlann, èistibh – Kids, listen

but NaaneeJi[10] said it was because they'd never gone away in the first place. The Scottish ones had missed being asked for favours and getting up to mischief. It made sense to her. Given how many folks were Christian, she'd half expected Jesus and all the Saints to appear, but much as the Vatican had tried to revive Latin, it hadn't happened. Given the cabal of available demons, that was quite a relief.

Cailean put his hand on the small of her back and leaned in. For a split moment she thought he was going to say something meaningful.

'Mo chreach,[11] John's over there, I'm going to see if I can borrow his big shears for the willow behind the fence.'

'Seach.[12] Ach, stay near in case the kids need us, okay?'

He was already turning away, John holding out a can of Tennent's Zero. She didn't mind. She reached up to adjust her woolly bonnet. A moment of regretting not having brushed her hair was left behind as the drone of the pipes caught the air. The crowd around her squeezed a little as the villagers moved to let the procession come in from the main street. The drum-roll echoed as it caught the walls of the square. This was no tight marching pipe band. This was wild ancient drumming. Someone whooped a high-pitched call. The response rang out from the other side of the square. The dancers were here. Light torches raised up above the people. The drums and pipes reprised their refrain, the calls and whoops responded, back and

---

[10] NaaneeJi – Granny
[11] Mo chreach – my dear
[12] Seach – okay

forth. In the crowd, heads turned to the sounds, as though watching a ball pass. As it picked up speed, folk began to join in. She was in a knot of people she only knew to smile to, though her friends and neighbours would be here somewhere. Was that Morna over there? No matter, she could feel the beat coming up through her feet, the pipes reverberating around the old walls of the square. Her body began to sway. Everyone around her had started to move. She noticed Old Bill call out a high 'yeuch!' and before she had thought to, she had called her own response.

Dressed in white, hair flowing, barefoot, the dancers were moving to the enormous pyre. The Bodach, for want of a better description a sort of anti-Santa – an old hobbled manlike creature meant to climb down chimneys to kidnap naughty children – appeared behind the dancers. Thankfully, it was just one of the village dads playing the part, though you never knew these days. It did seem that now the Albannaich[13] were using Gaelic more regularly, and the magic folk were settling down after their re-awakening, characters like the Bodach did not really come to take the children as long as they were reasonably provided for. Not much effort really, once the council had housed them, and the village clubbed together for a Netflix subscription. Of course, some had a neat side-line in making appearances. Not today though. The Bodach danced and leapt, pretending to scare the dancers back, but they reached the altar of Brìghde nonetheless. The lead dancer, last Beltane's May Queen, brandished a corn

---

[13] Albannaich – Scottish people

dolly the size of a toddler high above her head. A symbolic Summer Child, it was to be set alight and thrown into the pyre to start the blaze. The crowd immediately went quiet.

The Bodach lunged at the May Queen, she stared him down, eyes fierce, and with that, he slunk back into the darkness. The dancers crouched in front of her, and she followed their lead. She lowered the Summer Child to kiss its forehead gently before holding it in the flame of the candle on the altar. Head alight, she threw it as high as she could – a shooting star across the square. The corn dolly was now burning bright, the flames catching the kindling on the top. Shrina noticed the village Scout Explorers lighting the bottom of the structure too.

The Ban-draoidh, in her ceremonial robes, came forward to wrap her arms in a comforting gesture around the May Queen, who had fallen to the ground. Intentionally, of course – it was part of the show. Still crouched down, everyone around her started to hum and raise their arms up in thanks to the May Queen's sacrifice. She stood up, surveyed the crowd and, with immaculate timing, curtsied to the bonfire just as it burst into flame. The crowd leapt up as one and erupted into applause; the drums and pipes struck up. The May Queen was absorbed back into the throng of white-clad dancers, men, and women, and they swirled back out of the square.

Cailean had shifted round the square, no doubt having forgotten the arrangement to meet the children. So much for being a celebration of family love. For a moment, she considered the juxtaposition of the symbolic dolly sacrifice. Shrina would prefer the world to wither in eternal darkness over giving up either of her two, no matter how much they drove her nuts. Looking around, she noticed that the milk and sweets table was in a different spot than usual, which was sensible given everyone wanted a traditional quaich-ful to toast together. This part also seemed weird to her, sharing the May Queen's symbolic milk in order to have strength for the last storms of winter. The amount of shit she'd got at school for coming from a practicing Hindu family, as if an elephant-headed deity was any odder than this stuff. She did love it all though. Somehow this return of the creatures had allowed new Scots and old, no matter their heritage, to genuinely come together.

The crowds were thinning a bit, throwing their own corn dollies on the fire as they left. It was a cold night, but the majority of the village was still there, toasting with warm milk, 'bonny-bay', or bainne-uisge-beatha[14] – the whisky milk drink. Some would go on to join the performers at the pub, but most would head to each other's houses to celebrate love, friendships, and the return of the light.

Ah, there he was. Àdhamh was in the queue with his friends. She was not surprised. He waved cheerfully. They both knew she would not mind too much, it was Sorcha who was still a bit wee at seven years old to be left alone for an extended period. She walked over to him, pulling out some coins and his dolly.

'Here you go, a lurain.[15] We're going to the Bains's after. I need to nip into the shop for some bits. Where's your sister? Did she get a bonny bay?'

_____

[14] Bainne-uisge-beatha – 'milk whisky'
[15] A lurain – sweetheart

'A Mhamaidh,[16] she went to you a wee bit ago when I got into the queue after the dance.'

'To the tree? Which way round the fire?'

'Straight to you.'

'Fan an seof.[17] Get the milk, I'm going to look for her.'

Her phone was in her hand before she had even decided to use it. It rang and rang. Cailean probably couldn't hear it with the noise, and in his sporran he would not feel it vibrate. She sent a text to keep looking for Sorcha and the plan to meet and go to the Bains's. She stopped to look carefully around the square. There were children on the playsets on the wee green.

Something dashed past the corner of her eye. She felt a shiver down her neck. Thank goodness the fairies slept through winter. Never mind, she could not make out Sorcha in the group of weans. It seemed as though everyone she knew in the village was in her way.

'Hi, hi, yes it was lovely wasn't it? Always so moving. Have you seen Sorcha? No? OK, if you see her can you tell her to head chun a' bhùith?[18] Get her to wait there. I'm going to keep looking.'

She was starting to feel a pit in her stomach. She was still on the wrong side of the fire to make out the features of the children playing. As she skirted the fire, she noticed something was wrong. The flames had a green tinge, not like when you throw copper on it, the dark green. It seemed to pulsate. She could make out a shape. A body, legs, arms, a green person. She shook her head, must have

---

[16] A Mhamaidh – Mummy
[17] Fan an seof – stay here
[18] Chun a' bhùith – to the shop

been the Summer Child. Maybe there was something in the dolly. She carried on, but the shape remained on the edge of her vision, following her. Walking somehow. It was the wrong length for the dolly. It could not be. It was the size of Sorcha. The panic was rising up her gullet. She could feel the bad magic. She forced herself to look away from the fire. Dark forms were flitting around the top of the buildings around the square. No one else seemed to notice. They were moving faster and faster. Her heartbeat was picking up.

'A Shorcha! A Shorcha!'

She was moving faster. The rest of the crowd seemed to slow. It was as though she was running through one of those clips where everyone is in slow motion and the main character is moving normally. That would be the adrenaline.

'A Shorcha! Càite bheil thu?[19] A Shorcha! Has anyone seen her?'

No one seemed to notice her. The wind was picking up. If there was some weather coming in, then that should clear the crowds a bit more, yet no one was moving. At all – they were transfixed in place. The shifting flames were casting long eerie shadows. Unnaturally dark shadows. She started to step towards the playgreen, glancing back over her shoulder. There was Cailean by the tree. Àdhamh was at the same spot in the queue. The green figure in the fire had grown brighter. It felt hard to pull her eyes away. The wind seemed to be tugging at her but no one else was moving. Her scarf was being batted

---

[19] Càite bheil thu – where are you?

around her head, her coat flapping, and yet everyone was immobile. The dark shadows were racing around the top of the square, and the green Sorcha-sized flame figure was holding its arms out to her. The shadows were not connected to anyone. They seemed more substantial. Wraith-like. The hair on her neck bristled.

The green figure was human shaped in front of her. Her stomach lurched, breath tight. A face was formed in front of her very eyes. A face she had loved from the first moment, and she recognised every beloved feature as it morphed through the years. It was Sorcha, trapped in the fire. Reaching out to her. Screaming.

She reached out to her, the flames licked her skin and her body pulled back instinctively. The heat was sucking her face taught. She could feel the heat on her eyeballs, her brows singeing. Her chest was hot. She was reaching her hands out, but her fingertips were incandescent with pain. The dark shapes were whipping round her, wraith-like bòcain[20] pulling her hair, nipping at her, pushing her forward into the inferno.

Her leg was leaden as she dragged herself forward. The fire demon wanted her. The understanding swept through her brain. Like a warped Mughal Suttee rite, she was required and Sorcha was the lure. She rubbed her pendant.

'Goddess Kali, I must walk into the fire. Protect me.'

She felt just a little braver, enough for one more step. The tips of her toes were excruciatingly hot. She focused on Sorcha's face. She could do this for her leanabh.[21]

---

[20] Bòcain – demon
[21] Leanabh – baby

She took a breath, air searing her lungs, a sucker punch to the chest. One more step. She could feel the heat up and down her body, the cloth of her coat no longer providing any shielding. The Sorcha of the green fire, now an exact likeness of her own daughter, trapped in this blaze, opened her mouth in a shriek that resolved into clear words.

'A Mhamaidh, cuidich mi!'[22]

She threw herself forward to her little girl, only for strong hands to wrench her back.

'Sorcha! My baby! I have to free her!'

'I know. I will help you. But you will both be lost. I saw the Bòcain emerge. I had to make sure the May Queen was safe – they'll have been after her first. Oh dear, a ghaoil,[23] you're looking a bit crispy around the edges, here take a sip.'

It was the Ban-draoidh Ceana, changed back into her jeans and hoodie. She was holding out a cup of milk, the liquid surprisingly cool as it coated her scorched throat. Shrina did not know what to say. The rest of the people in the village still seemed frozen in place, their faces losing shape like melting wax. The wraiths were screeching around the square. Ceana was shouting through the wraith-wind.

'Sssh, listen. It is Sorcha in the fire, but she isn't burning. It's magic. We will get her. Before dawn. The others will come too when we call on them. We tricked the fire with the Summer Child. Listen, Shrina. You will need to be very brave for your girl.'

---

[22] Cuidich mi – help me
[23] A ghaoil – my love

Shrina nodded, trying to take it in.

She reached for her bag and emptied the contents onto the ground. Scrabbling through the contents, she lifted an item.

'Here is the obsidian amulet, hold it in your left hand. Good. You have an eight-wheel cross. That's been helping already, with Goddess Kali. She is a mighty one to have on your side. You keep her power in your third eye.'

She grabbed a flask.

'In your right hand, carry this water. Yes, normal water, we don't need a sacred well for this. Walk into the flames and say mo ghaol, an nighean[24], over and over. Throw the water over Sorcha, and the obsidian at her feet. An exchange. Wrap your arms around Sorcha. Tight. I will pull you back. Do not look back. Got it?'

Clutching the amulets in her hands, she summoned her courage to step toward the blaze. She pulled the image of the Goddess Kali from her mother's shrine to her mind and started to repeat 'mo ghaol, an nighean'. The flames were roaring at her. The searing heat repelling her. She could hear Ceana calling out ri solas Bhrìghde[25]. Desperate for support, she fought the need to turn back. Her shoes seemed to be melting as she stepped forward. Somehow the fire cooled, as though over a heat barrier. She felt a hand at her elbow. Cailean's voice shouting through the roar.

'Shrina, what are you doing? Come back.'

The urge to turn back into his arms and get his help

_____

[24] Mo ghaol, an nighean – my love, my daughter
[25] Ri solas Bhrìghde [*Breeda*] – by the light of St Bridget

was close to overpowering. He was pulling so hard it felt like the inside of her elbow being ripped. What if it was a firetrick? Her Cailean would have stepped in with her. She steeled herself. One more step.

'Mamaidh! Stop!'

The voice was Àdhamh. She knew it was a firetrick now, and yet he was harder to ignore. A white-hot triangle of tension formed between her shoulder blades. Sorcha in front of her, Àdhamh behind. She needed to turn, tell him to step back, away. Just as she wrenched her eyes from Sorcha's face, Ceana was shouting:

'Don't look back! It's not real!'

Keyed into the desperation in her voice, Shrina took another step. She was now in a glowing dome of flame, somehow at a comfortable temperature. The air was still yet her hair beat around her face.

Sorcha, glowing green, floating in the flames before her. Flipping the lid off the flask with her teeth, she threw the water, and the little girl crashed out of the air. Shrina's left hand was cramping. She squeezed tighter. Her palm felt sweaty. What if the obsidian slipped? She threw her arm forward to reach to her daughter, just as the very flames seemed to become hands to pull her back. She felt a jolt through her body. She had reached her girl but could barely grip hold of her.

She threw her whole body forward, her arms forming a protective cage. Elbows smashing on the embers, somehow not in pain, as though cushioned. She threw the obsidian to the flame hands on Sorcha's ankle. Immediately, they released her. Sorcha's weight sprung loose, and Shrina found herself rolling back, holding her daughter with every will in her body.

The wraiths were screeching around them, now drawn into the fire. Together, mother and daughter rolled back holding each other tight. The flames leapt around them, but it was as though they were in a bubble. Directly above, she could see the stars, but all around, whirling wraiths being sucked into the fire. She knew Cailean and Àdhamh were pulling her out. She could hear them shouting her name as they pulled, the distress in their voices searing her heart more than flames ever could. Snapped from their trances, all the people in the square rushed to them. They formed a human chain, linking together to pull them from the flames.

Each and every one, shouting, 'ri solas Bhrìghde'.

A rush of wind. The final wraiths sucked from the air. With a deafening woosh, the huge fire went out. In an instant, even the embers went as cold as the square's cobbles. The square was completely dark and still. Shrina was clutching Sorcha. For a moment, there was nothing else, as though suspended in the universe with her baby safe in her arms. Àdhamh and Cailean fell into them. They were complete, the family. She felt a breath of relief wrack her body.

Then, before she knew it, hands were reaching out, checking them, calling their names. Their village gathered, lifted them up and out, carrying them. Held up in their arms, safe. Shrina tried to look around over their heads, but Ceana was nowhere to be seen. She shook the idea she'd been swallowed into the fire from her thoughts.

'Mamaidh?'

Àdhamh's voice was questioning.

'It's done. Nothing is more powerful than people together. For evil or for good, the greatest power.'

Charlie Roy is the debut author of *The Broken Pane*, published 2021. Well known on the Scottish poetry scene, Charlie has performed at the BBC Slam, the Edinburgh International Book Festival, and Edinburgh Fringe. In prose as in poetry, her work focuses on women's lives, mental health, and family. Charlie was born in London and grew up in Spain, eventually trading the sunshine for Scottish wind, making Edinburgh home. She drinks too much coffee and loves long beach walks with her labradoodle.

HUTTON'S SECTION

Ash Caton

Signs of violence at the scene.
Charting scar and schism,
along a trail already cooled,
from King's Crag to Fingal's Cave,
he gathered the evidence.

In the palm, a clod of whinstone,
warming. He scoped the coalfield,
where, like marl, hypotheses were heaped,
and chipped away at the transverse,
dropping clues into the creel.

The wounds were plain, but of the war
his country couldn't speak.
Forces remained in the three realms.
Rumbles of the next action,
dismantling outposts of the last.

His case builds on a moving target
with no vestige of a beginning,
no prospect of an end.
The foundation keeps a layer
of faith, lucid in its flux.

Gaining ground, the sands recede
over wrecked Silurian ribs.
The body had been found.
An obscure light advances,
the old perspectives tilt and lift.

Here, he closed the circle,
brought the unconforming proofs,
and arranged them on the sill.
What was local and peculiar,
he made luminously general.

Ash Caton is a writer and bookseller who's been living in Edinburgh for six years. He's written and performed solo poetry for the Edinburgh Fringe, taken part in a Traverse Young Writers programme, and performed at many spoken word events in the city. As well as writing plays and poems, Ash produces a literary podcast called 'Ear Read This', which often focuses on local authors. His poem is inspired by the discoveries of Edinburgh geologist, James Hutton.

AGNES

Kirsten MacQuarrie

'Prick.'

The small army of men gathered around us gasps. He simply stares. Vision blurred from their blows, still I sense a pallor washing over his expression: an ashen wave of shame breaking before his hot, pulsing humiliation turns to rage.

'What did you call me?' Pale eyes peering, blinkless, he looms even closer than before. Cheeks stubbled; breath sour. We have been here for some time.

'They… ' The effort required to wrap my cracked tongue and parched, split lips around a full sentence makes my head loll slightly on my shoulders, dark walls spinning. My scalp feels lighter since they shaved it. My mind oddly untethered. By now, near extinguished by exhaustion, the sensation might be a pleasant one, were it not for lingering indents of the tight, braided binding that was thrawen at his behest around my skull. The men must have uncoiled it when I lost consciousness – no doubt worried that I would die before they had fully exploited their right to kill me – but the pressure still haunts my bruised, rope-burnt skin. A woolly ache clamps my temples: half hempbind, half handprint. I twist away from it and the memory, squirming until something rough snags across my collarbones. Not removed but only loosened, their rope snakes around my neck to form a noose.

'They… they pricked me.' Even muffled by swollen eardrums, I can tell that our audience is collectively holding its breath. Clearly, I owe some greater courtesy to this sneering, spoilt young man. An obligation of deference resounds faint within my weary brain. 'They pricked me, Your Majesty.'

One weighty exhale of relief released in unison. Are they incapable of independent thought? Still, I suppose communal stupidity does less damage than the way his twisted, whimsical mind works. Fearful. Irrational. Every woman in Scotland – England too, if his unsubtle power plays produce the result he desires – held hostage to his paranoia.

'And why was that, Agnes?' The shape of my name turns grotesque in his mouth, second syllable distorted into a hiss. 'Why did they prick you?'

Because you pay them by the hour, James. Because you, a cretin rich as Croesus, keep witch prickers on retainer in your bloated retinue of sycophants. Women would get the job done quicker, I might point out, if I could be persuaded to care about his kingdom's purse strings. Although he'll never know it, we do most of the work around here.

I stay silent. The time for cooperating in good faith – or conversely, for fighting back against ever-escalating violence – passed the moment the King's men stripped and searched me. Stripped, shaved, and searched me. And yet even no response seems to read as goading to this pampered prince. His weak, watery gaze stays fixed on me. 'Was it because of your mark, Agnes?' I feel every eye in the room dart downward. Bound by the ankles, I try and fail to cross my legs. A fresh draught of ice-cold creeps between my bare, bloodied thighs, the dungeon's dampness mingling with stagnant sweat – not all my own. But my body is the sole one on trial; my soul itself is damned to Hell for the crime of a single freckle that I never knew existed. Not until they hacked away at my hair down there.

'Was it because you summoned up storms to force back me and my bride?' Legs close to buckling, without space to fall, I feel James's words swirl and crest over me. Bilious as my stomach churns – already emptied more than once today – I think I nod, if only at the thought that his wedding should have never been sanctioned. She is fourteen. Just a girl. Tempest or not, young Anne should have escaped. To be trapped with this man is truly a fate worse than death.

Panting hard as if aroused by sheer exhilaration, he presses still nearer. A stale miasma of breath hovers between us. 'Was it because you brought the forces of evil into your village, abandoning innocent babes to perish?' If he means accepting the inevitable when it would save their mothers, then yes. Any midwife would say the same. In our field, although I cannot comment on witchcraft, the country is indeed on the cusp of change. A true ill wind if ever it blew. My time-honed and honoured profession is being shunned for smug, Kirk-sanctioned doctors: men – they are exclusively men – whose knowledge centres upon the certainty that they are paid to preserve hypothetical sons at the expense of fully-grown women. Not that Queen Anne is fully grown. Should the poor lass be carrying his heir, the child's child may very well kill her.

'Did you lie with the Devil, Agnes?' Dark though it is in here, those eerie, ethereal irises seem to glow with a ghoulish thrill at the prospect. 'Did you kiss his arse; take in his seed?' The King is touching me now, already he appears not to realise it. A rigid bulge prods hard against my exposed thigh. The sickness of hours past resurges deep in my core. Relentless, he stares, the blue betraying heat without any trace of warmth. 'Did you look the Devil in the eye, Agnes Sampson, while he claimed you as his own?'

'Yes.' This voice is not mine. It frightens me, almost as much as it does him. James's own tone falls to a hoarse whisper in reply, shocked as a tantrumming child whose screams must cease when even its wildest demands are exceeded.

'Are you a witch, Agnes?'

'Yes,' I repeat. The flash of fear across his face makes the lie worth it. 'I am, Your Majesty.' If his courtiers remain, I cannot see them. Cannot sense them. All that exists for me now is this man and what it will take to make him stop touching me. 'I know things.' A tart, metallic taste alerts me to the fact that my lip still bleeds from where his lackeys burst it. But I persist. A lowly subject like me gets no second chance at an audience with the King. 'I know Scotland is lost because of you. I know your vanity and vaulting ambition will see our country sold for pieces of silver.' Not supernatural; just common sense. Any fool can see it coming. Any fool but this one. 'And I know what you said to your wife on that first night in Denmark.'

James blanches. Truly feart. He should know how it feels before our encounter ends. 'Didn't you promise Anne it would be painless? That you would take care of her? Didn't you lie to your bride and swear you would be gentle?'

His fair lashes flutter rapidly. Agitated and, I hope, ashamed. 'How can you…?' The King of Scotland recoils from me, stumbling down into a clumsy half-bend in his haste to withdraw. Later, I will console myself with the thought that it looked like a bow. 'How did you know?'

Most men are the same.

When they bring me out, it appears morning is in mourning. Charcoal clouds shadow the castle walls; the cool grey horizon beyond is shrouded in mist. It may be my eyesight, of course, having not seen the sun in several weeks. Yet watched over and even embraced by this sorrowful Scots weather, I confess to feeling a little less alone.

Strong-armed by King's men on either side, seemingly afraid that I may otherwise take flight – if I could, would I have left it this late? – I am dragged on grime-steeped feet towards my pyre. Garrotted first, they tell me. Then burnt. A small mercy, maybe, or else a means of making certain that I am dead. Shivers start rattling the length of my tattered, stain-ridden nightgown, the singeing shame of this last indignity no match for January's frostbitten air. I suppose I will not be cold for much longer.

'Do you fear me, sir?' I ask the brawny, heavy-browed figure who must be my executioner. 'You should do.' A sudden spark of renewed courage courses through my veins, nerves flooded with perverse pleasure at defiance being the last thing I will feel. If my intelligence has infiltrated his sex's nightmares, if my body's abilities – magical only to those who misunderstand – have poisoned the shallow well from which these men draw their peace of mind, so much the better. The scales of our suffering can never be balanced.

The lad's thick fingers falter, fumbling for several seconds until a raw-cut strip of rope is held aloft. I think I hear him muttering a prayer. I myself should pray to God, to the Kirk's man, that he may forgive this sinner's soul. I wish instead that I was what they say I am. I wish I truly was a witch. I wish I had power to gather the forgotten women of the past, to call through the centuries to the unconceived girls of the future. I wish for my fate to echo in the soul of every female who walks this earth, the steely flash of sisterhood forged in vengeance even where no other commonalities bind us. I wish I could see their eyes glint, a million Eves with their hearts set alight by the fiery fury of reckoning against all that we are forced to accept as the bastard inheritance of the womb. Old kingdoms gone, not come; forsaking our fathers who art in Hell. The reign of man gone up in smoke.

Kirsten MacQuarrie is a Scottish writer and artist. Her first novel was *Ellen and Arbor*, released in 2020, and her second is the forthcoming *The Rowan Tree*, exploring the 'some-requited' love between poet Kathleen Raine and author-naturalist Gavin Maxwell. Although Kirsten confesses to being a born-and-bred Glaswegian, Edinburgh – and in particular the hidden stories of women in the city's history – have long been an inspiration for her, and never more so than in this story.

THE BUS STOP AT ARMAGEDDON

Allan Gaw

The heat hovered above the plain in a shallow sea of shimmering crystal. Along the dusty Highway 65, the bus, green and silver and catching the noon-day sun, was slowing. As it came to a halt, its hydraulics whined and wheezed it to a smooth stop. The driver pulled his lever to open the door, allowing a rush of desert heat to assault the near chill of the bus's air-conditioned interior.

'Megiddo. All change!'

'What do you mean? We paid to go all the way to Tiberias.'

The young woman had called out from her seat three rows back, but without looking, the driver shrugged and shook his head as he collected his things.

'This bus isn't going any further today, but you can wait here for the next one along. Everybody off!'

She turned and adjusted her headscarf while she muttered to her young husband in a dialect of Palestinian Arabic. But what was obviously the start of an argument was lost in the general shuffle of the other passengers rising from their seats to collect their luggage.

Among them was an American, who was struggling

to understand what had been said. He was unshaven, in his twenties, and carried all he had in a rucksack and was now appealing for some explanation of why they had stopped. His entreaties began loudly and grew louder in his vulgar attempts to be understood. Everyone on the bus could speak English, but no one was willing to be shouted at, especially in an American accent. Finally, the rabbi, who had been sleeping when the bus stopped, took pity on him and explained that they all needed to alight and wait for the next bus.

'But where are we?'

'Megiddo Junction. Not far from Tel Megiddo. You have heard of it?'

The rabbi looked the young man over and judged him to be sadly lacking any Jewish blood. Nevertheless, he smiled benevolently at the bemused gentile and patted him on his bare, but tattooed arm.

'It is famous in your Christian Bible. But you call it 'Armageddon'. I don't know why. That's not its name. But you always like to change things, don't you?'

The American had only heard the word, 'Armageddon' and brightened with recognition.

'Really! Jeez, that's in the Bible. And I read about it in the guidebook.'

He pulled his pack down from the rack and unzipped the front bulging compartment to rummage inside for the book. He pulled it out along with dusty socks and a half-eaten box of halva.

'Yeah, here it is. It's in the Book of Revelation – it's supposed to be where the last battle will be fought between good and evil at the end of days, when there will be time no longer.'

'If you say so, young man.'

'This place is so cool.'

'Unfortunately, not when you get off the bus. It's the hottest hour of the day, you know. So, mind how you go.'

Behind the American and trying to squeeze past him were two children – a boy of about seven and a girl of five. Their mother was calling on them impatiently to wait, but neither was listening.

The soldier watched the seven passengers step down from the bus, counting them one by one and checking their expressions as they each felt the thud of the midday heat on their faces. He had heard the bus approaching but had not even looked up from the piece of olive wood he was whittling with his pen knife.

He already knew this one would not be going any further. And besides, although he was leaning on one of the concrete bollards that had been placed to protect the bus stop from terrorist attacks, he was not waiting on a bus. He did need to get home, but a soldier on leave could usually rely on the sympathy of a driver to offer him a lift. All he had to do was wait long enough at the shelter.

From his dusty boots to his green uniform that could offer no camouflage in this landscape, to the green kippah pinned with a single hair grip to his short black hair, he was a tall reminder that this was a land perpetually at war. His kit bag lay on the ground between his feet, but his heavy rifle remained slung over his shoulder. That could never be put down. He was tired and bored by his wait and even the arrival of the travellers would hardly be a distraction. But then again, as they trooped into the shelter, he sensed something he had not felt for a while.

As soon as the American stepped down from the bus and saw the soldier, a young man his own age, he was cheered.

'Hey man, what's up? In the army, eh? Man, I don't know how you all do it. I mean, National Service. I can't imagine being ordered about and told what to do. But the kit looks good. What you got there? Is that a Galil? Looks like an M16.'

The American reached out to examine the assault rifle slung over the soldier's right shoulder.

'Don't touch the gun.'

The words were spoken with such slow, quiet menace that everyone now gathered in the shelter held their breath. The American did not have to be told twice and immediately backed off and put up his open palms by way of apology.

'Sorry, man. I didn't mean nothing by it. Just curious is all. Everything's cool.'

While the soldier went back to working the piece of olive wood in silence, the rabbi caught the American's eye and shook his head, half in disapproval, half warning. The American went back to looking the soldier over like a child sizing up a new toy in the window. He spotted the edge of what he thought was ink on the inside of his arm.

'Do you have tattoos as well? I have some cool ones. Wanna see?'

Without waiting for an answer, he pulled up his t-shirt to show the bald eagle on his flank. He then turned around and awkwardly with one hand tried to point out the map of Wisconsin on his back that he himself had only ever seen in a mirror.

'That's where I'm from, man. Not like here, not one little bit. What you got?'

The soldier laid aside his wood and pulled up the right sleeve of his tunic above the elbow just enough to reveal a simple black letter 'A'.

'Is that your initial?'

The soldier pulled up his left sleeve to reveal another symbol. This time it was one that the American recognised from his physics classes, 'Omega? Oh. I get it. That's not an "A", it's an alpha and that's an omega. Cool, what does it mean?'

'The beginning and the end. The first and the last.'

The soldier was watching the American intently as he spoke. When the young Palestinian man to his left shifted, a sudden ray of sunlight wiped the shadow from the soldier's face and for a moment he seemed to shine. The soldier searched the American's face for any hint of recognition but found none and quietly went back to his wood and turned his attention to the Palestinian couple who were still arguing.

She was angry with the bus driver, with the heat, with the delay but most of all with her new husband, whom she expected to do more to fix their situation. But theirs was a public row, with barbs hissed at each other under their breath – angry, clipped Arabic that was barely audible. However, the soldier heard it all and understood everything and concluded that their fight was not his. It would be resolved soon enough with tears and love-making as such tiffs always were. But what of the rabbi?

He was seated at the far end of the bench, overdressed

for the heat and trying to find enough shade to make the wait tolerable. He had leaned back against the all too secular graffiti scrawled on the shelter and was fanning himself with the book he was reading. The soldier's gaze was downcast, fixed on his carving, but furtively he would glance up to watch the old man with increasing interest. Could he be the one? When the soldier looked up the last time, he was met in return by the rabbi's gaze. Neither looked away, but both nodded in silent acknowledgment. The rabbi's head, however, was bowed a little lower than the soldier's.

The mother sitting beside the rabbi was trying to entertain her children, who were clearly in need of distraction. From her bag, she had produced a small cup and three dice and she was trying to make up a game simple enough, but at the same time engaging enough, to keep them all occupied. The rabbi could see she needed help, and he offered to take the strain for a moment. She smiled and thanked him for his kindness.

The little boy took to the game eagerly and grabbed the cup, covered it with one hand, and shook it vigorously in an attempt to extract the highest score from the dice. All he could manage, though, were two threes and a one. The rabbi said a little prayer over the dice before his throw but wondered if the sacred should be used in such a way to temper the profane. Then he smiled as he thought that surely there was no better use for the word of God. And he could not help exclaiming his delight at the five, four, and three he managed to throw.

The others, for want of anything else to do, began to watch the game. When the rabbi urged the little girl to have a go, she shook her head at first, but he coaxed her with a smile and a pinch of her cheek. To please him, she took up the cup, rattled it almost absent-mindedly, and then casually allowed the dice to spill out onto the concrete bench. They rolled off and into the shadows, and everyone had to peer to see her score. When the soldier looked up from the three perfect sixes in the dust and into the girl's eyes, he saw them filled with fire, and he knew.

'I've been waiting for you. Shall we play?'

The girl dropped her head and, in her shyness, tugged at her mother's sleeve to whisper in her ear.

'She wants to play tic-tac-toe. Have you got any paper?'

The soldier bent and pulled a book from his bag. It was battered and well-worn and was only being held in one piece by the seven elastic bands wrapped around it. The little girl took a breath as the soldier took off the first of the bands. There was a sudden, low growl of a motorbike in the distance along the highway that grew louder with its approach. The rabbi stood up to look out, and he could see the rider with the white helmet speeding towards them. The bike drew up at the bus stop, but the rider did not dismount. It was almost as if he was waiting for whatever might happen next.

As the soldier took more of the bands off his book, another three bikers appeared out of the heat haze in the distance. All were riding low, angry-looking contraptions, with twisted chrome and polished paintwork. The second drew up and stopped behind the first, and he at once took off his red helmet and shook out his hair. His leather jacket was emblazoned with images of tanks and exploding bombs and the American was already trying to get a better look, perhaps even a photograph. The third arrived a moment later and when he removed his black helmet, the small boy pulled at his mother to complain that he was hungry. She hushed him with a rebuke that was almost a bark, and he cowered in enforced silence.

The last of the four bikers was the strangest of all. He and his ride were completely covered in the fine white dust of the road, and he arrived almost as a pale apparition, while behind him the weather seemed to be changing. The cloudless sky was darkening in his wake.

'Now that they're here, should we start?'

This time the little girl's mother had spoken for herself, but almost at once she was given another whispered instruction and her tone changed.

'She wants to know if you would like to be a nought or a cross?'

The soldier tilted his head and smiled in puzzlement. The mother nodded and said, 'Of course. She just thought you might like a change for once.'

The soldier drew the grid of nine squares on the page and handed the little girl the pencil.

'Me, first?'

He nodded and, with a slight smile, she shook her head almost in pity. She took the pencil, carefully avoiding any contact with the soldier, and scratched her nought into the bottom right-hand corner. It was a perfect circle. Instead of handing it back, she placed the pencil on the paper. He immediately put his cross in the centre square, and the little girl could not suppress a sigh. The rest of the game was a simple battle of attack and block that led to an inevitable draw. The way it always did when they played, no matter who went first.

The child looked up and out at the bikers who were still waiting and then back at the soldier.

'Well?'

The soldier surveyed the sky above him and watched a bird fly high overhead. He also noted that the sun had already moved along its arc, and he said, 'Looks like we still have time. So, not today, but I expect we'll be meeting again soon.'

With that, the little girl heard the motorbikes kick into ignition. Revving loudly, they turned and went back up the highway in a convoy that disappeared again into the blur of the horizon. She looked tired and she took her mother's hand and said that she wanted to go home.

'We still have to wait for the bus, darling.'

As she bent to stroke the girl's hair and soothe the disappointment from her brow, the familiar sound of a bus coming to a halt caught her by surprise. Seemingly from nowhere, the Number 830 to Tiberias had drawn up and its doors were opening. The Palestinian couple rushed forward and were the first to board followed by the rabbi who was helped with his bag by the American. The mother lifted the boy on and turned to call her daughter. The little girl, however, took a moment to look back at the tall soldier.

He was still leaning on the bollard by the bus stop and already he had gone back to his wood. She could see now that he was not just idly whittling but was carving a delicate set of figures – a mother and a child. Her own mother called again, and as she was lifted up over the first high step of the bus, she took a last look at the soldier and could not help thinking he had his father's eyes.

Allan Gaw lives and works in Scotland. He is a pathologist by training and a writer by inclination. Born in Glasgow, he worked for many years at the University of Edinburgh. He has also worked in the NHS and universities in England, Northern Ireland, and the US. He writes short stories, historical crime fiction, poetry, and experimental novels. In 2022, he won the UK Classical Association Creative Writing Competition and the International Alpine Fellowship Writing Prize.

THE WATCHING

Anna Cheung

You gather outside as if mourning
at a funeral, shaped like black umbrellas
unfolding grief into the silent rain.

I sense a watching, the vulturing eyes,
hear whispers through the open window.
I sense you watching me watching you.

Time passes. But not by the clock,
where the seconds turn into minutes, to hours,
where the days turn into weeks then months.

Time passes by the wilting of irises
on the windowsill, by the arthritic curl
of my fingers, by my sorrowing spine.

Time dries up and withers away.
My muscles relax and my eyelids loosen;
I feel my flesh sink into the hollows.

Blood gathers, migrates to bruises.
I unbutton the skin, disrobe the body,
shedding the heavy carcass cage.

I step outside, slip inside your ranks,
become a member of the Watching.

Anna Cheung is a poet based in Glasgow. Her debut poetry collection, *Where Decay Sleeps* was released in 2021. Amongst other writings, her previous works were published in the anthologies *Haunted Voices* and *Forward Book of Poetry*, and literary magazines such as *Myth & Lore*, *Banshee Journal*, *Geist*, *Dreich*, *Koening Zine*, *Zarf*, and *Dusk & Shiver*. She was highly commended by the Forward Prize in 2022. She has performed at various spoken word events in Edinburgh, including the Edinburgh Literary Salon and the Edinburgh Book Festival.

PRAYING TO THE RESURRECTOR
(for Eurydice)

Ricky Monahan Brown

Every way I turn, I see ugly, contorted, inhuman faces, desperate figures trampling prone bodies. Kids are being lifted out of the crush on flight cases. Behind us, the crowd biblically parts as a skinhead wielding an iron bar he's torn out of a crush barrier pursues some kid, before it closes over them again and as the pyrotechnics pick out frozen frames in black and white and yellow and red. I can't tell if the mob is attacking the skinhead or falling upon the kid. The Rock God onstage is imploring the audience to make their way calmly to the exits, don't stop, don't look back, just keep moving calmly to the exits. I grab Emma's hand and we start for the exit signs etched in red at the far end of the arena.

We had met at the bar for the sad sacks and hardened drinkers, not that Emma was like the rest of us, she just wanted to drink somewhere she could read her book and not be bothered and if she had to, she could tell guys like me to get lost. And I didn't mean to bother her, but she looked like Justine except with dark hair and when the band came on the jukebox that one night, I saw her close her book and lose herself in the music and told her I had two tickets for the show, and I thought, oh god what if she really was Justine, what if Justine's soul had left her body that day we pledged our undying love on the beach and then had been trapped in the city haunting me, watching over me and waiting for the right vessel to inhabit and Emma was the right vessel because, you know, she really did look just like Justine and maybe that's why she liked the band so much, because Justine had chosen her as her host.

It had been the same song playing that day when she set our boombox down on the sand, slipped two tabs into her mouth and transferred one to me. I remember the slight inky edge to the taste of her tongue, which was usually simply subtly sweet. I remember how she held my head in her hands and looked deep into my eyes as if she was calling forth my soul to meet hers in the space between us.

'This is the last time, right? After tonight, we're grown-ups. We do things the right way.'

Stadium-sized disco drums broke over me in waves and I watched my bride dancing deliriously across the beach until the film skipped and jumped off its guides and bubbled and melted.

The band opened with that same song tonight, the big song. During the support acts, we had been moving closer to the stage and as things were about to kick off, we were no more than five rows from the front. I squeezed Emma's hand to let her know that I was there for her as the crowd heaved in anticipation, then let go as I felt an almighty pain on the back of my neck. Instinctively turning around, I was confronted by the man-mountain of leather and metal who had just put out his cigarette on me, smiling malevolently before moving into the new space that had opened up. I was relieved to find that I could easily recover Emma's hand. I didn't want to make that mistake again, didn't want to lose her. I couldn't understand why the crush had eased off so much until I saw the fights that were erupting all over the venue among kids that had carefully arranged their battles in advance.

Then the house lights were extinguished, the crowd surged forward again, the huge white drop curtain fell, and strobe lights flared and flickered, and a yet another tide of adulation crashed over the last. And now kids are getting pulled out of the crowd on flight cases. More freeze frames: a kid in a ripped t-shirt who had been riding across a sea of humanity that suddenly parts and drops him on his head; a man's grim exultation as he breaks another man's jaw for some imagined slight on his girlfriend; further back, a woman on her boyfriend's shoulders flashing her breasts to the stage; and, when I turn back to make sure she's okay, Emma's hand being ripped from mine by the tide as I am pulled down to the depths by the undertow.

I can't fathom time or direction as I scramble for the glasses that have been knocked from my face and I'm desperately trying to push what's left of them onto the bridge of my nose. I'm lifted to my feet to see yet more bodies of the injured and maimed and dead being lifted out of the pit onto the stage, and I'm gripped by the fear that my late wife might really be dead this time, and the conviction that this time I can't let her go without a fight, so I begin to battle back against current. I'm surprised by how easy it is at first. My feet are lifted off the wet, tacky floor and when I reach forward, I can grab handfuls of clothing and hair and flesh and pull myself forward, over, and through them. I ride the impact of one body, dip under another, bounce off the next, but I can't maintain my luck and then it is my turn to be dropped heavily to the floor.

When I look up to remonstrate with the raver who has let me fall, I am confronted by a woman who must be eight feet tall. Her waist-length hair is bleached blonde, her skin has never seen the sun, and her lips and sunken eyes are pitch black. She is out of her mind on bad drugs and I have interrupted the flow of her ecstatic frenzy. I immediately backtrack but already she has produced a katana from the black trench coat that skirts the heels of her black motorcycle boots, and steadied herself before wielding the sword in a smooth arc that cleanly severs my head from my body. The lights of the arena spin as my head flies through the air and I try to call for Justine, sing her our song, the big song, and I move my lips but I can't make a sound.

Then the lights stop dead, the house lights are up, the music has started again and everyone is dancing and everything is terrible and clear. The maenad lifts up my head by the hair and presents me to the stage like an offering, a sacrifice to the Rock God who's signing our song as he pulls Justine from the crowd like some rock star from the times when love was pure, and men tried their best to be good and honest.

Ricky Monahan Brown is the author of survival memoir *Stroke: A 5% Chance of Survival*, which was one of The Scotsman's Scottish Nonfiction Books of 2019. His Gothic novella *Little Apples* was part of the first issue of Leamington Books' Novella Express series in 2022. His short fiction has been widely published, including in Scotland, Ireland, and the United States. A regular attendee at the Edinburgh Literary Salon, Ricky lives in Edinburgh with his wife and their son.

YPRES

June Gemmell

23rd April 1915

Overnight we sheltered under shattered pieces of half-dead trees, leaves clinging to wounded branches. I couldn't sleep so I smoked and watched the stars overhead. I thought of my brother James, stationed in France, and prayed to a God I didn't believe in to keep him safe.

Now we stood in a silent line facing the German trenches. The 9th Battalion Royal Scots, bedraggled, but upright and in place. My numb fingers grasped the cold metal of my rifle, I could barely feel my legs and my kilt was heavy with dampness. I'd not had a proper wash for weeks and the lice in the seams of my uniform made me itch and scratch.

I'd stopped reacting when rats ran over my boots. There was one now nearby, beady eyes and long tail, sitting confident as you please. Sammy Moffat stamped his feet and the creature scuttled off, splashing its way through the water pooling at our feet. I nodded my head to Sammy. In comradeship more than confidence. He'd been wounded in the fighting north of Ypres before Christmas. Bullet in the leg. Been sent home to convalesce for about five minutes. And here he was back again, poor bugger. With a grudge to boot.

I whispered, 'Moffat, you okay?'

'Aye Lawrie. Top-notch. We'll get the bastards today, eh?'

The shelling had stopped, and all we could hear was the distant booming of field guns miles down the line. The last few days, we'd been so close to the enemy trenches we could hear their voices. God knows what they were saying. Probably complaining about the cold. Cadging a roll-up. Just like us.

A shout echoed out across no man's land. A sharp burst of a gunshot followed close by. I looked down the line for Captain McDonald who stood poker straight, hand held up, whistle in his mouth. Another shot rang out.

The barbed wire was supposed to have been cut last night by the outgoing C company. We had to hope it bloody well had. I didn't want to stick my neck out to look. I'd seen too many men cut down, head and helmet rolling down the line like a bowling ball.

As a third shot rang out a somersaulting shape hurtled over the parapet and landed at our feet. There was a brief flurry of surprise, and the men closest stepped instinctively back. I stared at the unfamiliar grey uniform.

Sammy Moffat was first to gather his thoughts.

'It's rainin fuckin Germans.'

Moffat's lean body was tight with tension. He raised his rifle and the steel of the bayonet stopped inches from the German's chin. He addressed him. 'Well Fritz, good to meet you at last.' He raised the butt of his rifle higher. The German's hands crept above his head.

Captain McDonald pushed his way up the trench, checking his watch. 'Back off Private.' He nudged Moffat roughly and indicated the stranger should stand up.

Davie Alexander, who could speak a bit of German was called for. He stood beside the captain and barked, 'Wie heissen Sie?'

'Brandt.' The German spoke in a thick accent, alien to our Scottish ears.

Alexander searched his mind for the right words. 'Warum sind Sie hier?' He pantomimed Brandt's catapult into the trench.

The German launched into a long speech, with Alexander nodding his head from time to time. No one moved. Alexander turned to the captain. 'He's handin himself in. There's hardly any troops back there. Most of the regiment's gone to fight somewhere else. He's had nothin to eat for days.'

The captain shook his head. 'I don't like this. Could be a trap.'

The German started to weep. Fingernails full of the Flanders dirt, he tried to pass around a photograph of a young woman. No one responded. His trousers were torn at the knee and the stain of dried blood made a wreath around the gap.

The day was losing light, and the captain looked at his watch. 'Time to advance. Alexander, and you Lawrie,' he tapped my shoulder, 'stay here. Watch the prisoner. Everyone else, positions. Over the top. One minute.'

The sky gathered its pale colours and waited.

The shriek of the whistle sounded. Men scrambled up the slope, boots sliding in the mud. The guns started up, whether they were ours or the enemy's we didn't know, and below in the trench, we were showered with earth and debris. Alexander and I tried to press ourselves into the side wall of the trench, but Brandt sat on the wet boards and clutched his head in his hands, muttering all the time words which were unintelligible, given the exploding sky above our heads. We kept our guns pointing at him, all the time watching with one eye for more Germans appearing over the top.

In a brief lull, the German raised his head. To Alexander he said. 'Wie heissen Sie?'

Alexander hesitated, then pointed. 'Me, Alexander. Him, Lawrie.'

I watched the German chew on his dirty fingernails for a while before he spoke again. He had to shout above the guns. 'Und wo wohnen Sie?'

I looked at Alexander.

'He wants to know where we're from.' He yelled 'Edinburgh.' He had to repeat it a few times, the German cupping his ears as bombs whistled and sang above us.

'Ah, Edinburgh, ja, ja.' He nodded as if this was the best place in the world to come from. He laid his palm on his chest. 'Ich komme aus Bamberg.'

I waited for Alexander's translation.

'He's from Bamberg.'

'Where's that?'

'Don't ask me.'

The German searched in his pocket. He waved a post-card at us showing narrow buildings and cobbled streets. He nodded at the picture.

'Bamberg.'

I said nothing. Alexander nodded distractedly, eyes returning to the direction of the German lines.

'Mein Vater hat eine Braueri.' He pointed at a building in the photograph. 'Hier.'

I nudged Alexander.

'He says his dad's got a brewery.'

I laughed out loud. 'Tell him, tell him, I work in a brewery in Leith.'

I mimicked drinking a pint of beer and pointed to myself. The German laughed. Whether he understood or not I didn't know, as rather than translate my words, Alexander spat into the muddy water.

The air above us shivered with noise.

I imagined another time another place; a warm Edinburgh pub, glass windows lighting up the inside with a rose-coloured glow, glasses full of amber beer. My brother sitting opposite me laughing, head thrown back the way he did, thumping the table, beer glasses spilling. But here I was in this freezing hole in the ground, damp seeping into my bones. Death hanging in the air.

Alexander's shout wrenched me from my thoughts. Our boys were on the way back. The first few were triumphant, clutching tins of food and German helmets. The ones that followed guarded a ragged bunch of prisoners, eyes darting left and right.

It turned out Brandt had spoken the truth. Most of the German regiment had retreated, leaving only a handful to defend their trench. They had fought like mad dogs our boys said, injuring a number of our battalion before being shot dead or, if they were lucky like this lot, rounded up as prisoners. Sammy Moffat paraded up and down the trench like an idiot, wearing his plundered German helmet.

Brandt was ecstatic to see his compatriots and launched into a thick dialect of welcome in a tearful speech. The half dozen of them sat huddled together, watching us with apprehensive eyes.

It had been some time since I'd had a proper meal. We'd rigged up some tea in our billy cans earlier, but supplies of food couldn't make it through because of the shelling. Now, some kind of fruit cake was being passed up the line. 'Cake' was definitely the wrong word. Hard, dry, main ingredient God knew what, but it was good to have something in our stomachs.

Alexander boiled some water on the stove. The hot can of tea steamed into the cold air, and I burned my hands holding it. I noticed no tea was being passed to our prisoners and when I mentioned it Sammy Moffat grabbed my arm.

'Are ye jokin me? They should be fuckin shot! Or starved to death. Slowly. That's what they deserve.' He lifted his gun.

'Moffat. Weapon down!' Captain McDonald made his way towards us. 'Send for Alexander.'

'I'm here sir.'

'Tell the prisoners to stand.'

Alexander did this and they stood, mud and blood stained, a pathetic sight.

McDonald addressed them in English. 'You're going up the line. Back to Potijze Wood. From there, A Company will take you onwards. Alexander, Moffat, go with them.'

'If they try to escape I shoot them, sir.'

McDonald held Moffat's gaze. '*If* they try to escape you shoot them, soldier. If they do not try to escape you do *not* shoot them. Got that?'

'Aye sir.'

We could hear the taunts and jeers of our men further up the line as the German prisoners made their way back to the reserve trench. The voices got louder, then sounds of a scuffle reached our ears. A single yell sliced the air, then the crack of a rifle silenced all other noise. One shot. Just one. All was quiet except for the boom of shells, on the other side of Ypres.

No one acknowledged the shot. At my feet in the muddy wetness was a photo of a German girl, plait wound around her head. I picked it up. I couldn't read the German words, but the name Hilda was written at the bottom. I slipped it into my pocket.

June Gemmell is an editor for Loft Books. Her short stories have been published by Loft Books and Soor Ploom and the magazines *Gutter* and *Razur Cuts*. She is working on her first novel *Loose Change*, featuring an Edinburgh school janitor who wins the lottery, but keeps it a secret. She has also written a children's novel. Born in Edinburgh, she lived there for many years before moving to the Scottish Borders.

DAWN

ALTERNATIVE LIFESTYLE

Julie Galante

Sandra approaches the well-kept suburban home. The flowerbeds and lawn are geometric in their precision; automatic sprinklers lie in wait, ready to water but not today, not when guests are arriving. Francine is too good a hostess to forget a detail like that.

She pauses on the front porch and assesses the nervous humming of her body. She could just go. She could turn around, run away home. Never look back. It isn't too late, yet.

The door opens, and Laverne is there greeting her warmly. 'Francine's just in the back getting everything ready,' she explains. 'Let me take your coat.'

Sandra steps inside, admiring the hardwood floors and flocked wallpaper of the vestibule. Her shoe – a sensible heel – knocks against something small, which rolls away making a tinkling sound.

'That'll be your house soon.' Laverne smiles knowingly.

Sandra commands her face to smile back. 'I guess it will.' She hands Laverne her coat and smoothes down her dress.

'Big day for you! No going back to the way things

were after today. Are you ready?' Laverne gives Sandra an enthusiastic shoulder squeeze.

'I think so.' Sandra reflects for a moment. Is she ready? This time last year she was trying to recombobulate herself after her fiancé had fled three weeks before the wedding. That heartbreak feels so remote now – and is something she need not feel ever again – according to Francine.

Francine can be very persuasive.

Sandra knows she needs a change. She is so tired of it all: the swiping, the false hope, the ghosting, the bitter disappointments. She needs to take action. Yes. Yes, she is ready.

'Fabulous. Come through to the lounge. We're having refreshments before the ceremony.'

They walk through a set of double doors into a bright, plush living-room furnished with overstuffed seating and polished woodwork.

'Sandra! Darling!' Francine, flanked by several other women, looks radiant in a flowing orange and yellow caftan, a long brown braid wound around her head. 'Oh my dear, I am so happy for you. This is the first day of the rest of your life.'

Sandra chokes down a nervous giggle, which turns into a snort, as they embrace. 'You have the most lovely home.'

'All part of the lifestyle, my dear. All part of the life-style. You'll find yourself no longer spending money on evenings out or fancy holidays. Plus, with all the free time you would have spent worrying about a relationship, you'll be able to focus more on your job, really get ahead.

Remind me what it is you do again?'

'Editing. Freelance, mostly from home.'

'So perfect. You'll get to spend all day with them! Cup

of tea? Nip of brandy? I'll be right back.' Francine drifts away to find the tea cosy.

'You are going to love him,' a woman with a frizzy halo of red hair leans over and stage whispers to Sandra.

'Oh yes. I helped pick him out – he's perfect,' adds Laverne. 'I remember my first. Not long after my second divorce – maybe three months. He helped me heal and brought so much joy. Now I have six!'

'I started with two older ones – a brother and a sister. They needed so much love, and it was as if the universe intended for me to be the one to give it. They deserved it so much more than my bastard of a cheating ex,' says the red-haired woman.

'I tried dating for a while after my husband passed, but it was a shitshow,' says a woman wearing pointy glasses and several bulbous rings. 'I don't say it enough, but I am so grateful to Francine for bringing me into the fold. Speaking of, it looks like she's ready to start.'

The women turn their attention to Francine.

'We will head into the ceremony presently. But first, please raise your cups and glasses.' Francine glances proudly around the room. 'To our newest member! May your hoover be powerful and your home flea-free.'

'Hear hear!' The assembled group of a dozen women reply in unison. They finish their drinks and move across the room to where Francine is handing out hand-knit shawls of various ombre colours. Once they are all wrapped up, another set of doors opens, and they enter a shadowy room, lit only by a smattering of scented candles.

Inside, the women form a tight circle. A low humming emanates from somewhere close. Sandra stands in the centre, not knowing where to look, unable to make out individual faces in the low light. A woman steps forward and hangs an amulet around Sandra's neck.

The humming gets louder and more engine-like. It seems to be coming from all around.

Sandra feels dizzy. Suddenly, Francine is standing before her holding a silk pillow with a small creature on it. The animal, white with black splotches across its back, lets out a weak mew.

'Aaaaw!' gasp the assembled women.

Francine hands the pillow to Sandra and says, 'I hereby welcome you to the Ancient Order of the Ladies of the Cat. May he be your first of many.'

'You can never have too many,' chant the other women.

Sandra takes the pillow and examines the kitten. Her heart grows full with its cuteness. She knows in that moment she was right to come here, to join these courageous souls. She looks around at the others and smiles.

Afterwards they adjourn to the lounge for cake and more drinks. Sandra sits on a large sofa, the kitten curled up asleep on her chest.

'So, how do you feel?' asks Laverne.

'I feel… complete.' Sandra sighs, glancing down at the warm ball of fluff.

'That won't last long,' says the red-haired woman. 'You'll be hankering after your second in a few months.'

'Psst, Eleanor, let her enjoy this one a while first!' Laverne hits her playfully.

'I'm just saying – one is never enough. This lifestyle is all-consuming. Which reminds me, I better get home to my brood. I don't like to leave them for more than a few hours. They miss me too much.'

As Eleanor stands to go, Sandra's eyes catch the scratch marks that crisscross her forearms.

'Oh yes. Mine get downright surly if I'm away too long,' says Laverne. 'God forbid I go away for a night – I know to expect pee in my shoes the next day.' She glances over at Sandra as she's speaking. 'Oh, but don't worry! It's all worth it.'

'It is, absolutely,' says the woman with the pointy glasses and rings. 'Even if some of Francine's rules seem puzzling, they're all for our own good. You don't want to end up like poor Pam…'

'Shhh!' hisses Laverne, looking around. 'Don't let her hear you mention that name.'

Sandra fingers the new amulet hanging around her neck, noticing how smooth the stone is, how heavy the chain. She makes a mental note to ask Laverne about this Pam woman later, when they can speak freely.

'It's a cat's eye.' Laverne pulls a similar necklace out from inside her shirt. 'We all have them. You're one of us now.'

The kitten opens its eyes and looks at Sandra in terror.

Julie Galante explores relationships, the uncanny, identity, and grief in her fiction, creative nonfiction, and visual art. For her, writing is a way to make sense of the world and to forge connections with others – she enjoys being able to make people laugh or view life in a different way. She lives in Edinburgh, and loves living in a city with such a thriving and welcoming literary community, including the Edinburgh Literary Salon. Julie's artwork and writing can be found on her website.

EXOTIC FIONA

Catherine Simpson

Mothers gather at the school gates, 1972.

Her name was exotic: Fiona.
She wore sandals on leathery feet,
browned by a faraway sun,
not heels from Clarks
with American tan
like other mothers.
Her hair – a thick plait –
thrown over one shoulder
was streaked and moonlit,
like woven quicksilver,
not tinted and set,
with a scarf or a net.
Her skin was soft; sun-drunk,
golden, warm to the touch,
fine-lined and aglow.
Her billowing smock; jewel-bright,
(the first with no pinny pulled tight)
danced at the school gates,
as my mother, and the others, gathered
arms knotted, over cardis, to wait
and watch this outsider, this incomer.
But Exotic Fiona got lost in her books,
in her gingerbread house,
full of ideas; a 'mature student',

huffed the mothers,
as her children arrived uninvited
for tea; sticky hands,
dirty feet, which everyone said,
was frankly, a cheek.
Like her quest for lentils in the shop –
a fruitless search – among tin after tin,
of mandarin and peach.
She settled for Cox's Orange Pippin.
Was she a hippy? Maybe.
We'd seen one on *Look North*.
She smiled and pushed the pips in
among the herbs; pressing the earth
to wish them well,
as we watched, edging nearer;
bewitched by Exotic Fiona.

Catherine Simpson is an Edinburgh-based novelist, memoir-writer, and poet. Her novel *Truestory* was inspired by raising her autistic daughter, Nina. Her memoir *When I Had a Little Sister* explores the death by suicide of her sister, Tricia. *One Body*, her second memoir, examines growing up and growing older in a woman's body and is structured around Catherine's year with breast cancer. Her dramatic monologue *Driving Dad to the Old Folk's Home* was broadcast on BBC Radio 4. She is a long-time friend of the Edinburgh Literary Salon.

HERE LIVED

Pippa Goldschmidt

Our destination is an address on *Schumannstraße*, in the Westend district of Frankfurt and very near the conference centre which hosts the annual book fair. On a warm and sunny Sunday morning in June, about forty of us meet outside this large, late nineteenth-century house that once accommodated a single family and is now subdivided into several flats. More precisely, we cluster around a patch of pavement which has been covered with a square of red velvet and strewn with rose petals suggestive of a wedding. But this is not a joyful occasion.

Many of us have travelled a long way to be here; we have come from America, France, England, Sweden, Italy, and Ireland. A few of us have settled in Germany; in Berlin, Bremen, and here in Frankfurt itself, but none of us was born in this country. The oldest of us is 85, the youngest around 14. Some of us are at ease here and can speak German fluently, others have never been to this country before and are only here out of a sense of duty. We do not share a common language, nevertheless for some months now, with the help of Google Translate, we have been exchanging emails, discussing arrangements, and making plans.

I know a few of these people but I'm feeling shy, and so I stand quietly listening to polyglot conversations around me while I wait for the ceremony to start. Perhaps I am the odd one out because I have travelled the least, I'm currently staying just a short tram ride from here in the south of the city. As I stand and wait, my stomach begins to knot with the anticipation of what will happen. I didn't expect to feel nervous; it was only when I left my flat that I realised I was attending a memorial service. The three people we have come here to remember died many years ago, however, for two of them this is the closest thing to a funeral that can be arranged.

I moved to Frankfurt at the beginning of 2020, arriving here shortly before Covid. When people ask me why I left the UK for Germany, I mention Brexit and my desire to live in a country that still believes in the value of being connected to its neighbours, and that willingly takes in refugees. This is true but Brexit is also a cover story that masks other, more deep-seated links. My grandfather grew up in a town just outside Frankfurt in the early years of the twentieth century; when he left school he was conscripted into the German army and fought on the Western Front in the First World War, before returning and working as a lawyer in an office less than a mile from where we are standing today. His was a large and extended family but there is nothing left of it in Frankfurt now. Nothing apart from me, and sometimes it can feel very lonely to be the last to bear a name in a place where that name was once so common.

A man who appears to be in charge claps his hands

and announces in German that the ceremony is about to start, and my cousin Daniel pats me on the shoulder; a comforting gesture that makes me feel included. The square of red velvet is whisked away and we are shown the purpose of our gathering; three brass plaques set into the pavement, each engraved with a handful of words.

The man explains the purpose of these three *Stolpersteine*, now a common sight all over Germany and elsewhere in countries which suffered under Nazi rule. The word *Stolpersteine* literally means 'stumbling stones'; devised by the artist Gunter Demnig in 1992 to honour the victims of Nazi persecution, each one records the names, births and deaths (when known) of an individual. Each one starts with the phrase '*Hier wohnte…*' (Here lived…) to make us think about the lives of the victims before we are confronted with their fates. The purpose of placing each *Stolperstein* outside the last known address where the victim voluntarily lived (as opposed to a ghetto) is to remind people that persecution happened everywhere during the Third Reich. It didn't start in prisons and camps, but in houses that continue to exist to this day long after their former inhabitants fled or were forced out and transported to their deaths.

I'm too far away from these *Stolpersteine* to read what they say, but I know they record the names, births and deaths of a mother and daughter who were murdered in Auschwitz in 1944, and of a father who fought in the French Resistance and who survived. Lotte Mentzel *née* Rothschild was my grandfather's first cousin and she had three children. The eldest daughter, Ruth, was transported with Lotte to Auschwitz on the very last train to leave before Paris was liberated, but the younger daughter Catherine is here at the ceremony today, and reads the eulogy. Catherine is 85 years old and has had to live nearly all of her life without her mother and elder sister. Nevertheless, she tells us about their lives. Lotte grew up in this house with her parents and her three sisters before she moved to Dessau to study at the Bauhaus school, where she trained as a metal designer and met Albert Mentzel. Ruth was born just a few months after their wedding, 'a magnificently large "premature" baby', as Catherine says. When the Nazis seized power and the Bauhaus was shut down, the family fled to France where two more babies were born. During the Nazi occupation and Vichy regime, each of the children was baptised before being hidden in different French families, but Ruth was staying in an area that became a war zone after the Allied invasion of 1944, so Lotte brought her back home to apparent safety. Before she could be hidden elsewhere, the Nazis discovered the two of them and deported them to Auschwitz.

Catherine's speech is not just a memorial to her destroyed family, it is also a powerful condemnation of fascism and of the weakness and complacency in democratic systems that allows them to be overrun by people who hate and discriminate. She is also critical of the idea of 'roots', the idea that we have our origins in a particular place that must therefore be idealised; 'roots are a concept that is too often weaponised against migrants, refugees and travellers. We come and we go. What is important are the stories we tell about our pasts.'

Catherine is a reminder that the victims of the Holocaust were not just those who were murdered but are also the relatives who survived. There are still many people like her who have had to live nearly all their lives with unbearable loss.

Lotte Rothschild crops up in various histories of the Bauhaus, and she and her husband are the subject of a famous photo taken in 1930 by Etel Mittag-Fodor (see Bild-Akademie.de). In this image Lotte is wearing work-clothes and her hair is cut as short as Albert's; as she leans back against him, he holds her with his arms stretched out in front of them both as if explaining something, his hands blurred with movement. The photo appears both studied and spontaneous; the composition can either be read as two people modelling architectural principles, or as the portrait of a couple at ease with each other, who trust in each other's support.

Lotte's work complements the metallic nature of her memorial. It is common practice amongst Jewish families to honour their dead by placing stones on their graves. But it seems fitting that Lotte's stone is brass, a metal she must have been intimate with when she worked at the Bauhaus, helping to design and build table lamps, kettles, door handles, and other household appliances.

A *Stolperstein* costs 120 euros, and until the actual ceremony I had assumed that close family members had paid for the three being unveiled today. But that is not the case in Frankfurt, where relatives are forbidden from paying for *Stolpersteine*. Instead, other people with no direct connection to the family volunteer to pay. Now, during this ceremony, two people standing amongst us are introduced to us as the donors of the *Stolpersteine*, and we clap them and their altruism.

These *Stolpersteine* are not actually the only physical

memorials to Lotte and Ruth in this city. Frankfurt's Holocaust memorial is an array of small slate plaques set into the wall that encircles the old Jewish cemetery. The gravestones inside the cemetery were damaged and broken up by the Nazis, and are now unreadable. In contrast, the Holocaust memorial meticulously records the names of each of 11,908 victims who once lived in Frankfurt. When I go there, I find my own surname written over and over again, confronting me with the fates of my relatives, and reminding me what a Jewish city this once was and is no longer. The history of this place, written on brass and slate and stone, and distributed around these streets, is weighty. It can be crushing to be a survivor.

Stolpersteine are ubiquitous in the streets of this city; as I walk around my neighbourhood I can nearly always catch one out of the corner of my eye. The brass tarnishes quickly but it is common to see a *Stolperstein* newly polished and with a small candle of remembrance set nearby. Especially on the 9th of November, the anniversary of the November Pogrom in 1938 (formerly known as *Kristallnacht*) when nearly all synagogues in Germany and Austria were attacked and thousands of Jews sent to concentration camps. *Stolpersteine* function individually as well as collectively, creating an expanding network of remembrance and atonement.

After Catherine's speech, Daniel starts Kaddish and some of us join in. Kaddish is a prayer for the dead that does not mention death and that cannot be said alone, it requires a minyan, a group of at least ten adults. Saying Kaddish is inherently a public act, an affirmation of the mourning process. As Daniel leads the prayer, I look around and see faces at windows, watching us.

Schumannstraße is a quiet street, the people who live here can't be used to groups of Jews lamenting the deaths of their relatives.

When the ceremony is finished some of the group walk away, I had assumed they were also relatives but it turns out they were not. Perhaps they don't know any of us, perhaps they simply felt an obligation to be here. This is a reminder to me that the group is not homogeneous; it has brought itself together for a specific purpose and will now disperse back to its homes and, in our case, to a restaurant for lunch. The man from the local *Stolperstein* organisation who has organised today's ceremony must also rush off, he has to attend two more. There is a big backlog because of Covid.

Later, after we have eaten lunch, Catherine hands each of us a small present. She has made little booklets out of recycled paper and card, and personalised them with our names handwritten on the cover. These individual notebooks feel like a counterweight to the *Stolpersteine* and they are the most appropriate gift, because what else is needed other than a book to write in, to record what has happened?

Pippa Goldschmidt is an author based in Edinburgh and Berlin. In 2020 she co-edited *Uncanny Bodies*, a specially commissioned anthology of fiction and essays about Freud's uncanny, as it relates to health and illness, forests and cities. She has had her work broadcast on BBC Radio 4 and published in *Mslexia*, *Gutter*, *ArtReview*, *BBC Sky At Night* magazine, *The Times Literary Supplement*, *Magma*, *Litro*, and *The Real Story*. You can find out more about Pippa on her website.

A DAY IN NOVEMBER

Mary Byrne

November again. The Castellani Dance Academy's Show, and it would be the last time Yvonne Reeder would star. At seventeen, she was the school's oldest and most advanced pupil, the one with the most Royal Academy certificates. Next year, she'd probably be studying geography or biology or any other subject that wasn't dance and in another part of the country. Or – if she failed her A levels – she'd be waitressing in a hotel down the road in Blackpool.

'Castellani'. It sounded so romantic, so far away. The place where dreams were made. Yvonne had thought so once, even when she was climbing the rickety stairs to the studio at the top of the old canning factory. She'd looked up the word. In Italian, it meant 'the governor of a castle'. The school was the castle and the principal, Mariella, the governor.

Yvonne helped prepare the studio for the evening. The chairs, borrowed from the church hall across the road, had been stacked at the door by willing dads. The trestle tables were folded up in a corner, brightly coloured skirts for the national dances draped over one of them. Mariella had changed into a gold lamé dress and dangerous stilettos and, unable to help, was giving directions from a bench at the front. She'd had her hair dyed black and styled into a bun, backcombed, and lacquered.

'Put the tables out first, Yvie,' she called. 'Then the tea urn and stuff from the corridor.'

Nobody else ever called Yvonne 'Yvie'. She wouldn't have let them, but she admired Mariella more than any other person. The first time Mariella had called her that – she was only ten or eleven – she had winced but not complained, and so it had stuck. Yvonne knew that Mariella Castellani's real name was Mavis Catterrall but she never told anyone.

Yvonne and some of the older girls carried the tables across the room and pulled out the legs. Three of them lifted the urn, already full of hot tea, onto a tabletop. In a box, they found crockery and several bottles of squash. They arranged the chairs in rows up to the dance floor. Miss Hubbard, the pianist, opened the piano, set out her music, and played a few notes to warm her fingers.

Mariella lit a cigarette. 'Leave enough room for people to get through,' she called. Her lipstick was white and gave her a ghoulish appearance.

In another country about which nobody in the Castellani had given any thought that day, the President of the United States and his wife were on their way to Carswell Air Force Base for the short flight from Fort Worth to Dallas, Texas.

Yvonne had time to think while she worked. Who would be coming to see her? Not her Mum, that was certain.

Mum knew about it, but had told her last week – 'giving you lots of warning so you're not upset' – she would be ten-pin bowling in Blackpool with her new boyfriend. 'It's early days, love, and he might be "the one".' Her mother thought every new boyfriend might be 'the one' at the beginning. 'You wouldn't want to spoil that.' The last sentence was a statement, not a question.

Helping at the school in the evenings and weekends as well as attending classes, Yvonne didn't have time for a boyfriend. All her leisure was dedicated to dance, not going to youth clubs or coffee bars.

Maybe Grandma Jean would come. She'd have to get the bus from Cleveleys and she wouldn't like waiting at the bus stop in the dark, but she was still a more likely fan.

Mariella was probably her greatest fan. Mariella believed in her, even gave her free extra coaching for exams. Alright, Mariella used her as unpaid help as well, but she was the only reason Yvonne had reached this far. The star. When she was younger and had understood less, she had thought this must mean she could progress to the Royal Ballet School's White Lodge in Richmond Park and train to be a professional ballerina but, as well as needing money to do that, you needed talent, a huge amount of it. She might be the best in town but, taking part in competitions, she'd discovered she was a minnow in a very large pool. Years of trying to be a dancer and where had it got her? Arranging tables and lifting tea urns. And then there were her A levels. She'd spent so long in this place she'd hardly done any revision.

'You could be a dance teacher too,' Grandma Jean had said. 'You're as good as that Mariella. I know who she really is.' And Grandma had touched the side of her nose.

The difference between Yvonne and Mariella was that Mariella had money. She'd married a trawlerman when she was sixteen. When, or if, your husband returned, he had good wages and with some of that, she had rented the studio, bought the piano, and paid for advertising. If anything went wrong with the school, well, she still had her husband's pay.

She tried to concentrate on the evening and not worry about the future. Make sure everything and everybody was in the right place, then do her best in her solo. She carried the skirts for the national dances along the musty corridor to the big changing room that had been the factory canteen. The tiny tots were already in there putting on their regulation black leotards and soft shoes, the grans helping. They would go on first – so that grandmas could rush them home at the interval and straight to bed.

When she returned, the audience was beginning to arrive: dads, mums and grans – but mostly mums and grans – all in their Sunday best. Her mum wasn't there. Neither was her grandma. Mariella stood at the entrance, smiling with her white lips, and taking money.

At five to twelve, the plane arrived in Dallas. The President and the First Lady settled themselves into a convertible for the motorcade drive downtown to the Business and Trade Mart where he would give a speech. The rain had stopped, and the sun had come out. They wouldn't need the 'bubble' roof.

At the Castellani, Yvonne led the tots from the changing room to the studio and onto the dance floor. After some hesitation and giggling, the little girls showed off their knowledge of first to fifth Positions, and then did some simple steps, ending with twirling round to the right on tiptoe. Two little girls twirled to the left by mistake, but the audience laughed and clapped anyway. Back in the changing room, Yvonne helped the national dancers into their skirts, and handed tambourines out to the ones doing the tarantella. The pupils tripped eagerly down the corridor after her. She put her finger to her lips to silence them as they neared the studio.

Miss Hubbard began a catchy Italian tune. The tarantella dancers ran round the floor, energetically shaking their tambourines. Mothers and fathers cheered. The Hungarian czardas dancers followed. Miss Hubbard played a melody, slow at first, then faster as the girls folded their arms, stamped their feet, and snapped their heels together. Their red and blue skirts whirled around with them. The audience clapped in time to the rhythm and shouted 'hooray!' when they'd finished.

It was seven o'clock and Mariella announced the interval.

'Go and get yourself ready,' she whispered to Yvonne. 'I'll do the tea urn.'

In the changing room, it was chaos. The national dancers were pulling off their skirts and putting on their outdoor clothes, while the senior girls, who would go on before Yvonne's solo, slipped into leotards and soft shoes. They would do a lyrical dance but not on pointe. That was Yvonne's forte. She sat, trying to shut out the noise, waiting for everyone to leave. The smell of unwashed bodies pervaded. It was hot work dancing and not all the pupils had the luxury of a bathroom at home.

When the younger pupils finally left to meet their

parents and the senior ones queued in the corridor waiting to go on, Yvonne put on tights and a pink leotard,
and bent to tie the satin ribbons of her pointe shoes. She
pulled on a pink dance skirt, then pinned her dark hair
into a tight bun. In the mirror, she was slim, graceful,
every inch a budding ballerina. No, she wasn't. She was
the star of a second-rate dance school in a town that no
one at White Lodge, Richmond Park, would ever have
heard of and, if they had, would be horrified to learn
about. Docks, fishermen, old factories: these weren't the
elements of a prima ballerina's life. A prima ballerina
would jet from capital to capital, dancing but also going
to concerts and dinners, meeting the world's most cul-
tured people.

She was a failure. The school was a failure, mediocre,
even if she had passed all these exams. She had wasted
most of her teenage life. No boyfriends or friends would
be coming to see her, and not even relations. Maybe she
could go home. No one would see. Just put her clothes
back on, tiptoe along the corridor and down the stairs.
Mariella would make excuses about a sudden ankle twist
or a stomach pain. Maybe one of the other senior girls
could do a solo. There would be a bit of a fuss tomorrow,
but she could live with that.

She got ready anyway, unable to decide. Her pointe
shoes clumped like clogs on the wooden floor. When she
went into the corridor, the senior students had finished
and they filed past her, faces flushed, eyes sparkling.

'Good luck, our star!' one of them called breathlessly.

She felt herself blush. How could she let them down,
the other dancers? They still had hope, and they all
looked up to her. She reached the end of the corridor

and glimpsed through the door. No mother or grandma but more people, all chatting excitedly. She would have to do it.

Mariella was hushing everyone, and seeing Yvonne, gestured for her to come. She walked onto the dance floor, head high, back straight, arms gracefully by her side. Miss Hubbard began to play the medley, beginning with a waltz.

She had only danced for a few minutes when there was a commotion. Some dads had arrived and were whispering loudly. Others were saying 'Shh'. She heard the words, 'Oh no!' and 'Don't tell them!'

Was a trawler late and missing? Many of the dads and grandads were trawlermen, as well as Mariella's husband. It was so easy for a boat to capsize when iced up. Her heart, already beating fast, burned inside her.

Out of the corner of her eye, she spied Mariella walking over to the men, then turn, her face as white as her mouth. It must be a trawler.

She should stop, but the audience, oblivious, smiled encouragingly, their faces glowing under the lights. Miss Hubbard, intent on following the score, played on. Yvonne went through the steps automatically, without feeling, all the time trying to watch the group at the door.

More people arrived. More whispering. A ripple of movement in front. Mariella was coming towards her, a hand raised for her to stop. The audience fell silent. Mariella faced them. A lock of hair had come loose from her style and swung wildly.

'Ladies and gentlemen...' Her voice shook. 'There has been a dreadful incident in the USA.' No one moved. 'President Kennedy has been shot.' Gasps. 'There are rumours… there are rumours that he has died.' Several women cried out.

A gust of wind blew in from the stairs. Yvonne shivered. The beautiful young couple so far away. Everybody knew who they were; everybody at school admired them and followed them eagerly on TV. They were going to put the world to right, to stand against tyrants and for justice. She didn't quite know how they were going to do that, but everyone knew they were. She wanted to cry too but all the people out front could see her.

After the first silence, the audience were talking animatedly to each other. The rest of the performance would surely be cancelled. Who would want to watch any dancing after this? It was like the end of the world.

But Mariella had started speaking again, this time in a sharp, lively voice. 'Ladies and gentlemen, this is a tragedy, but whatever's happened, we must let Yvonne finish. She is our star, our hope. This is her last year and the last time we'll see her.'

The audience hesitated, but when someone shouted, 'Hear, hear!', others joined in.

'Could we have a round of applause for Yvonne.' Mariella walked to the side, clapping, and the audience, after a pause, clapped too.

It didn't seem right to dance, almost a sin, but the people were all staring at her, expectant, as if she could save what had been lost. She had to try.

She took up her position on the dance floor. Miss Hubbard began the waltz again. This time, her body seemed part of the hypnotically beautiful music, moving with its pulse rather than her own. Her pirouettes on pointe were smoother, even with her left foot; her sissones were higher than she'd ever jumped and more exact. She glimpsed the audience, eyes wide, following her. In the middle of a turn, she saw her mother sitting on the floor, cheeks tear-stained, eyes red, smiling up at her. Next was the adagio from Sleeping Beauty: stately, majestic. She held the arabesques and développés without shaking. She was not afraid to dance slowly. Every movement seemed effortlessly graceful as if she was Princess Aurora.

The final piece was the lively mazurka from Coppélia. She skipped and clicked her heels. The audience swayed in time to the beat. A man in the front row even hummed. Mariella signalled for her to repeat it.

She finished. There was raucous cheering and foot-stamping. Someone shouted 'Bravo!' and others joined in, standing. Her mother ran to hug her.

Mariella, who had never done such a thing before, kissed her. 'Prima ballerina!' she cried, taking her to the front.

Going down the corridor to the changing room, she could still hear the cheers. They had trusted her with their hopes. She was a dancer.

Mary Byrne is a writer and artist who lives in Leicestershire but part of her schooling was in Edinburgh. Her short stories have been published in magazines and anthologies and she is also working on a historical novel. She says her art is narrative and her writing visual! Mary won the Leicester Writes Short Story Prize and was shortlisted for the H.E. Bates Short Story Prize in 2019. She was Highly Commended in the Frome Festival Short Story Competition in 2021.

FOUR CUPS

Tracey S. Rosenberg

Everyone at our seder table has a cup – one cup
to drink four cups of wine.
This is how we celebrate Passover as free Jews,
because slaves don't drink wine, or at least
    they don't
drink wine from cups, certainly not *these* cups,
silver and embossed with grapes. Aunt Rivka
    announces
she brought these cups from the Holy Land.
    Grandpa's face lights up.
Uncle Samuel sighs and smiles. 'Rivka doesn't
    mean Jerusalem;
she means Saks Fifth Avenue.'

There's a cup for every one of us, seventeen
    this year,
crammed around the table with all the extra
    leaves in,
just enough space for Grandpa's wheelchair.
There's a special cup for Elijah, the prophet
    who went to heaven

in a chariot made of fire. The horses drawing
    his chariot
are also made of fire, and maybe that's why
    Elijah only sips from his cup.
Not for fear of getting drunk – if you were a
    prophet who ascended to heaven
but still visits every seder in the world, you
    can hold your liquor! – what I mean is,
what I *mean*, Uncle Isaac, if you'd let me *finish*
    already,
if Elijah downed wine like a frat boy and
    sprayed droplets everywhere,
he might splash the horses of fire. They'd twist
in their blazing harness, hissing and writhing
    and expiring in wisps. Then Elijah
would have to trudge across the world on
    foot. He'd never get to our seder on time.
Then how would we know about freedom?
Mom brings out her special prune compote in
    the etched glass bowl.
The little kids say 'yuck' and grab handfuls of
    chocolate macaroons.
Aunt Judy peers over her glasses and says, you
    always put in too many apricots,
and Mom says, oh and because Bubbe left *you*
    the cookbook,
that makes you the world expert on compote?
And on they go, same as every year, till the
    rest of us pound the table
and sing about the little goat.

Are we on time? We're on the third cup!
Do we care if little goats are made of fire?
I bet Saks Fifth Avenue doesn't even sell
  chariots.
Benny and his girlfriend slipped away while
  we searched for the afikomen. *That's*
  freedom.
Grandpa's poking at his compote with a fork.
  His shirtsleeve rode up.
He has so many age spots,
you can hardly see the numbers anymore.

We all drink wine from cups! We aren't slaves.
  Not slaves at all!
Not here, not any of us anywhere.
We sing and drink until we forget, and then
  we understand.
We are horses and apricots and cups blazing
  with fire.
Aunt Rivka, what a joyful silver cup.
It's the fourth cup.
Here, take Grandpa's cup and pass it on –
tell that lightweight Elijah to fill it to the
  brim.

Tracey S. Rosenberg is the author of a historical novel and four poetry collections, including *The Soup of My Ancestors* which, like 'Four Cups', focuses on Jewish heritage. She's won a New Writers Award from the Scottish Book Trust, and recently spoke on BBC Radio Scotland about how to deal with rejection. She was previously Writer in Residence at the University of Edinburgh.

A NAME NO MOTHER WOULD GIVE YOU

Chiamaka Okike

Everything showed on Kirimah. When she was younger, it made it easy for her dad to name all the scars he gave her. 'Disobedience' ran from her ankle to the middle of her calf. 'Unrelenting stupidity' was a zig zag across her forearm. 'Yan ludu' was just a slap. It didn't leave a mark – for longer than a week anyway – but it was the only one that felt like a truly permanent etch.

Kirimah tried to remind herself that they were from the past and that she had fresh injuries to focus on. She could only hope that this one would be free of scars. She had been mostly still as Salimah worked around her face with mini ice-cubes that she'd tied in a black nylon bag, but Kirimah was never prone to silence for long.

'Hajiya won't be happy that you're wasting the ice.'

Salimah dragged the cubes across her face, a slight pause was her only indication that she'd heard anything.

Kirimah bristled at being ignored and pulled away. 'I'm fine. Go and put the rest back in the freezer.'

Salimah leaned forward so Kirimah leaned further away. 'I'm serious, Salimah, Hayija won't be happy.'

Salimah pulled her in by the shoulder and placed the makeshift ice pack firmly back on her face.

'Then she can take it out of my pay.' Salimah shrugged. 'And she will.'

Salimah shrugged again, aggravating Kirimah further. 'Daina. Stop!'

Salimah halted, pausing before she let the black nylon bag sit behind them on the bench.

'Your face is turning red. Tomorrow it will be purple. The next day, green. Why are you fighting me? Let me…' Salimah reached for the ice and then her face. This time Kirimah caught her hands firmly and gently lowered them.

'Salimah, I'm okay.'

Salimah turned away as if she had been slapped and not simply refused. Eventually, she turned her body back toward Kirimah, opening and closing her mouth slowly until she finally let the question slip out. A question that was never much farther than the tip of her tongue from the moment she met Kirimah.

'Who did this to you?'

When Kirimah had first strolled into Sabon Gari, clad in a dark blue niqab and darker blue eyeshadow, her immediate answer then would have been 'my dad'. Despite walking confidently, her stride was slow, hiding a limp acquired from an angry man with unfortunate access to a heavy wooden stick. He had hit her… because he could. But that time in particular was because Kirimah's quiet refusal to marry was a sin worthy of death to him. She'd focused on her religion as much as anyone should in her father's opinion. She'd gone to Mecca (twice!). She observed all the prayers – even the one in the afternoons. She didn't curse, drink, or gamble. When she wasn't at home, she was polishing shoes in a quiet corner of the market. The most exciting her day got was Tanimu. Sometimes, she imagined that the most exciting her life would ever get was Tanimu.

But it wasn't enough for her father that she was – if the whispers in the neighbourhood were anything to go by- perfect. She needed to be perfect… and a husband.

'Who will eat from your trade!' He had shouted at her that day. 'Are you not a man?! Will you not marry?'

Her whisper, 'I am not,' was enough for the first crack of the stick against her leg. At first, she thought the liquid wrapping itself around her leg was 'disobedience' re-opening and setting itself up to be an even worse scar, but it was just urine. She thought how pathetic it was that her bladder refused to hold anything in the face of fear… in the face of her father.

If the pain hadn't seared itself through her and clawed around her vocal chords in that moment, she would have corrected herself. She might even have tried to make a joke. She had never known her father to be a particularly bright man, but even he could draw a straight line from the kohl, faded lime bra, and red lipstick that Kirimah had kept carefully hidden under her bed – and the three unmistakeable words she had just uttered.

'The—,' her father had started then stopped; for once, dumbstruck. In the absence of words, he raised the stick high and aimed it towards Kirimah's face. 'The girlfriend you bought those things for, you will marry her. I don't care if she is a karuwai. I don't care if… I don't care! You will marry her this week or…'

He didn't finish the sentence, and he didn't need to. It had been a simple and effective method of threatening since Kirimah was young. It was in his silence that he did his most damage. He let the stick drop to the side and took large strides out of the room. Kirimah counted his steps and waited till she got to eight before attempting to stand upright. The pain that shot through her nerves had her kneeling again. With great care she picked herself up to make her way to her room. There, she waited until it was dark before slipping on the bra, and niqab, and with greater care, applied the midnight blue eyeshadow and rose coloured lipstick. Those items and her limp were the only thing she carried to the nondescript brothel run by Hajira Kubra all those months ago.

To her credit, the Hajira didn't make her start earning her keep until the six-day mark. Kirimah was throwing up against an unpainted, brown brick wall after her first customer when she met Salimah. She had offered Kirimah a sachet of water and given her the three hard thumps on the back that taught her the first and most important lesson of the brothel – 'stand up'.

Kirimah couldn't complain too much about a life that granted her access to education, crude entertainment, and, on the very rare occasion, an attractive man.

'Da'ud.' Was Kirimah's answer.

Salimah gathered her hands to her mouth in shock. Kirimah resisted the urge to roll her eyes at her friend's naiveté.

'No! Da'ud has been here. He would have recognised you. Maybe he didn't see it was you. Maybe—'

'He has seen me, Salimah.' Kirimah leaned back on her hands. 'He has seen me in more ways than one.'

'But then… no. No. He would never hit you if that were true.'

Kirimah laughed, she couldn't help it.

'Do you think…' She could barely finish the words through her laughter. 'Do you really think the men who come to visit us are men of honour? Why? Because we hail them "Alhaji Alhaji?"'

'Be respectful.' Salimah chastised.

Kirimah simply shook her head.

'We call Kubra "Hajira", but she doesn't even bother fasting in the holy month.'

'Hajira—'

'Is the only person in the whole Zaria who is honest. And if respect was measured by honesty, then she is the only one in the whole Zaria who deserves respect!'

Because Kirimah had raised her voice in a way Salimah was not used to, she shrunk down in her seat and began playing with whatever was left of the ice cubes.

'I'm sorry, Salimah, I didn't mean—'

'I know you and Allah… I know you abandoned God, but please try to be respectful.'

It was Kirimah's turn to look away. She wished she had her own black nylon bag to toy with. Salimah's words were crueller than she could possibly realise. Kirimah remembered one of the days she had donned her blue and red make-up combo and snuck into a nightclub. Weary of dancing, she stood outside the building for a smoke break. Even though it was an hour deemed sinful and unacceptable by most, a woman clad in yellow and green roamed the streets. She spat on the spot on the ground closest to the floral slippers Kirimah had chosen to wear that night before beginning her rant.

'You are… you're an abomination! You and your kind are why God lives in heaven and doesn't come to earth. Out of fear… out of disgust for what his creation has become.'

Kirimah leaned down and put out her cigarette on the spot where the green-yellow woman had spat. By the time she came back up, the woman was gone. In the seconds that she'd stooped and risen, she had a flashing epiphany. God was all she had ever known. And before Tanimu, all she had ever loved. The woman, to insult God, brought a burning rage to her throat. To insult God because of her felt like a whole different type of burning. A violent flaying from the inside out. She decided then and there that no one would ever have the chance again.

'God has nothing to do with me.' She said it out loud. Her last prayer.

'Let's leave God out of this,' was all Kirimah could manage then.

Salimah uncharacteristically agreed.

Her relationship with God confounded Kirimah on most days. Salimah was staunch in her belief that he was forgiving, possibly even accepting, of all that she did – because he was accepting of her. She envied Salimah for it. For the fact that one day she could leave the brothel, leave Zaria, and become something completely different. With water and whispered words she could become whole again. She could stand in front of God and man with a shrug and say, 'I was a prostitute, but I'm not anymore.' And that would have to be it. She would have to be allotted mercy because karuwai is not a permanent state. It's not a death sentence in the way femininity or queerness is. Kirimah didn't bother with salvation because she knew there would be no redemption in the cards the universe dealt out for her. There's no crevice in the world she could run to where she wouldn't be a woman. There could be no 'was' for her.

'Is it already time for Alhaja Salimah's sermon?' Maimuna said, squinting at her bare wrist.

Maimuna slapped Salimah's back to elicit a reaction. She was rewarded with a growl, and an arm lashed out at her. Maimuna grinned and took it in her stride, straddling the bench as she inserted herself into their conversation.

'What is the topic of our sermon today? A prostitute's guide to salvation?'

Salimah frowned in the way that she always did right before accusing Maimuna of using words to intentionally confuse her. In their compound there was an older karuwai who had been a teacher in what she described as 'a past life'. Having been unable to kick the habit, she hosted unofficial lessons in one of the bottom floor hotel rooms that were normally empty in the afternoon. Maimuna was inarguably her best student. If it was a good week, Kirimah was a close second. Though Husaina (or Ms. Husaina, as she preferred during school hours) was trained as an English teacher, she also took it upon herself to impart lessons in history, literature, and biology. It was where Maimuna picked up words like 'salvation', and subsequently why Salimah – who didn't make it a point of duty to attend lessons – frowned at them.

It was the second time that day that she surprised

Kirimah when, instead of the down-turning of her lips and up-turning of her nose, she asked, 'What does salvation mean?'

Clearly the question came as a shock to Maimuna as well because she didn't answer immediately.

'It's about—' she started, then stopped. 'It's about being saved.'

'How?' Salimah was quick with the question.

Kirimah had the answer to that. When she was ten years old or so she'd committed what she considered her first sin. She'd been in the marketplace and a much older woman had stumbled and fallen – spilling her merchandise on the floor. Kirimah had stopped to help her pick up the items. But in doing that she'd also stuffed a caramel coloured bra into the satchel she'd been carrying that day. Later that night, when her dad and stepmoms were asleep, she'd tried it on. It was a ridiculously loose fitting C-cup that slipped down to her waist and refused to stay put no matter how much she tightened it, but still. Of all the things she could have felt then, irritation was at the forefront. Why didn't the bra fit her? And why did the misfit aggravate her so terribly? It took her five more years to reconcile the anger, hurt, and confusion of that moment, and she used the clarity to steal a bra that did fit. It was lime green and an A-cup.

In the moments that she'd dress up – stuffed bra, floral slippers, and chestnut wig – she'd feel what the Christian missionaries, who her father routinely chased away, had come to preach. They spoke of a feeling and a place that was in equal parts freedom and sanctuary. They spoke of a saviour, blue eyed and blonde haired, who would take them there. All they had to do was confess, come clean, be true. If she ever did turn back to God, that would be her defence.

'They told me to be honest and I am!' She would scream to the heavens.

She thought that maybe if she shouted it in her high heels, in her denim mini skirt, in her pink crop top that brought out her collarbones, He would listen. Because in those moments she couldn't be closer to sincerity – and salvation, she had learned, was about truth.

Maimuna shrugged, 'You pray, you fast, you live a clean life and hope it's enough for God.'

Salimah shook her head, disbelieving.

'Anyone can do that. That's not—'

Maimuma cut her off with a soft gasp. She had just noticed Kirimah's face. Her first instinct was to reach for it, but just before making contact Kirimah pulled away.

'Who did this!'

Kirimah ran through the same pattern in her head again, reliving her father, then Da'ud, then the men that had stood by his side under the mango tree that somehow always had overripe fruit.

'Everyone.' She let out without thinking.

'In the market? In Zaria? Kirimah, who exactly?'

Kirimah was not unaccustomed to her friend's bursts of energy or anger. She'd seen it the first time one of the other women had asked Kirimah whether she was hiding a penis under her skirts. Maimuna had come alive with enough rage that the woman had never asked Kirimah that (or any other question) ever again. And of course, Kirimah appreciated it, but she secretly wondered whether Maimuna did it because she found her personally endearing. Did Maimuna think, don't bother my friend Kirimah who is pretending to be a woman, or, don't bother my friend Kirimah who is a woman.

She never asked of course. She didn't think there was anything an honest answer would add to her life outside of more hurt. She counted herself lucky that the women either called her 'yan daudu' when she was out of ear shot, or said 'Kirimah' in that sickly sweet tone that told her she was being mocked.

'Da'ud.' She answered finally. 'And... and some of his friends. I don't know them all – Balil, Gambo... I didn't see them all.'

'I'll kill them!' Maimuna loudly declared.

Kirimah laughed for the second time that evening. She reached over for Maimuna's chin and rocked it back and forth slightly.

'They'll kill you first.'

Though Kirimah had meant what she said, the layers of anger in Maimuna's eyes spoke of a lethal conviction and almost made her eat her words.

'Why did Da'ud hit you?' She paused, reconsidering. 'Was it Da'ud?'

'It was Balil, on Da'ud's behalf.'

'That dog? What could have provoked him enough to unleash his pet on you?'

Kirimah rubbed her neck.

'Kirimah,' Salimah perked up, her interest piqued all over again, 'what did you do?'

'He...' Kirimah gestured at empty air. 'You know I can tolerate it when the women here say it, but not them. Not him.'

'Yan daudu?'

Even then Kirimah flinched at the words.

'Yes,' she said simply, hoping her discomfort didn't come through in her voice. Apparently, it did.

'You are still afraid of that word? Still?' Salimah asked. All signs of her worry had given way to genuine confusion.

'Yes.' Kirimah doubled down. 'I've told you I don't like it.'

Salimah laughed and the sound lit Kirimah up with rage. Even Maimuna turned to her in shock.

'You're laughing?' Even though she was angry, Kirimah's voice only held wonder.

'Why won't I laugh? Who likes yan daudu? Who likes karuwai?' She had stopped laughing but her voice was still laced with amusement. 'If you don't like it, nobody can call you it. Simple. I know your mother didn't call you Kirimah, which name did they give you?'

'My mother is dead.' Kirimah said through gritted teeth.

'Did your father remarry?' Salimah asked conversationally, apparently oblivious to Kirimah's boiling.

'Yes.'

'And those women, don't they have children? When they were picking names, did you hear any of them say Kirimah? Where would they have heard such? The name is not even Hausa!'

'Salimah—' Maimuna tried to intercede, feeling the waves of anger rolling off her friend.

'Maimuna, stop babying her,' and then she rounded back on Kirimah. 'Wherever you got the name, you're the only one that bears it in Zaria. Me, when I first came here and Hajira used to call me 'Safiyah', I refused to hear her. The only day I answered her was when she called me 'Salimah'. She lifted her hand in the air as if exasperated by the situation. 'You are not yan daudu but someone will say "yan daudu!" And you will turn around as if your name is not Kirimah. Or is your name not Kirimah? Do you want to change it again?'

Despite herself, Kirimah laughed. Salimah had an unintentional humour about her.

'No, I'm not changing it again.'

Salimah, as if struck by a brilliant idea, turned to Maimuna and hit her lightly on the chest.

'Yan daudu, how far?' She had deepened her voice by a few octaves, evidently role-playing as a man.

Maimuna stuck out her hand in Salimah's face.

'It's Maimuna to you, Alhaji.'

'Ah okay, let me go and meet your sister, then.' She turned towards Kirimah. 'Yan daudu, how far?'

Kirimah appreciated the sentiment, but she had a darkening bruise around her eye socket to serve as a reminder that this was just play-acting.

'They'll kill me.' Kirimah said gently.

'They'll just laugh.'

Kirimah felt her anger flare up again.

'And that's better!?'

'Better than death, yes,' Maimuna volunteered.

Kirimah stood up.

'At least they think you're a woman! You would… You'd never understand.'

Maimuna stood up alongside her, her stance issuing a challenge.

'Yes. What could two karuwai know about the fear of death? Men would never mock us, beat us, or kill us.

We are here for enjoyment. We didn't see kilishi to trade like other women. We *wanted* to pull down our pants every night for 350 naira and a place to sleep.' Maimuna stared down Kirimah, chest heaving. 'You are my friend, Kirimah, and I would never say that to you. I would never dare to say that you don't understand.'

Kirimah collapsed onto the bench, suddenly drained of energy.

'I don't want to die,' she said quietly. 'And if I have to die, I don't want it to be those men that kill me.'

Maimuna sank like she did, watching her warily from a distance on the bench. She and Salimah locked eyes.

'Aminiya, you're not going to die.' Salimah said and rubbed her back. Her tone was as soft as the gentle circles that she stroked into her skin.

Maimuna was far less soft.

'We won't let them kill you.'

She offered it with no comfort or mildness. She said it like it was a fact. A truth. She said it like she would say 'the sky above us is blue but the sun is so bright we can't see it,' or 'the bench beneath us is brown but the sand has turned its legs a dusty red,' or 'you cannot be killed because we will not allow it'.

'And,' Salimah added, as if she'd just stumbled on a eureka moment, 'they've enjoyed you too much to kill you.'

Kirimah laughed semi-bitterly before she spoke.

'When I was a —,' she cut herself off and began again. 'Before I came here, I had this barber that I used to go to – Muhtari. Sometimes I still see him in town. When I would go to get my hair cut, he would always be playing something on his small TV. One day it was Pan... Peter!' She snapped her fingers together. 'Peter Pan. Him. And

I remember that green girl, a fairy, 'Tink' or something. When the movie ended, Muhtari finished laughing, shook his head, and changed the channel. Do you know what he said before he changed the channel?'

The women looked at her with anticipation.

'Sosai wawa.'

Both Maimuna and Salimah looked confused so Kirimah continued.

'Those men… they think I'm Tink. They think I'm a fairy. They enjoy me when I'm gold like her. Small like her. Funny. Naked…' She sighed. 'But they don't think I'm real. They don't think I'm real at all, and when I make myself too real, I get this.' She gestured at her bruised face. When they don't like me… when they get tired of watching me…'

Salimah began rubbing gentle circles in her back again and even Maimuna squeezed her hand briefly.

'And maybe I am just like Tink and like those other children on Muhtari's TV. Because once I stop being a fairy for them I know, like Peter, that I'll never grow old.'

Salimah sighed and pulled her hand back.

'How many times does Maimuna have to say it?'

Kirimah nearly recoiled at her tone. Gone was the softness that had characterised her voice and touches. It had been replaced by a steely anger. Even Maimuna seemed shocked.

'Enough of this Pan and Tink talk. Enough of the "they could" and "they will". Touch me.'

Kirimah stayed unbelievably still, forcing Salimah to reach for her fingers and lay them across her lap.

'Maimuna, touch her.' Salimah instructed in that same harsh tone.

Maimuna, unlike Kirimah, responded quickly, though the shock in her eyes held an undercurrent of bewilderment.

'Look at your hand.'

All their gazes turned towards where Maimuna's fingers had brushed Kirimah.

'Look at my lap.'

Again, their gazes trailed to where Salimah directed.

'Do you see gold? Glitter? Juju?'

Kirimah had gone from shock to downright confusion.

'You're not a fairy, Kirimah, you are just a woman! You will die, but only when you have wrinkles, like Hajira, and your voice cracks when you shout at the yarinya. It will be a life that will not end with any of us in Heaven, but it will be long, and that's what you want.'

Kirimah nodded slowly at the outburst.

'I also want…'

'I mana.' Maimuna held a hand in front of her face, 'just live first.'

Chiamaka Okike is the author of the short stories 'Songs about Surulere', 'If People are Art then Museums are Graveyards' and '14 Lasts Forever', as well as the essay 'Amore E Liberazione'. She grew up in Ibadan, Nigeria, and enjoys long walks, and a love of literature, which is now fuelled by the Edinburgh Literary Salon. It was on one of these walks that she started thinking about how queer people never get a community, or a place where they can gather authentically. It led her to write about Kirimah, a trans woman in a northern Nigerian brothel.

CHURCH AFTER LOCKDOWN

Suzanne Smith

Gathering here is
Different now. You can
Tell by the way the bricks
Arrange themselves, the way
Stained glass shines on a faith
Changed in isolation.
It's been months
Since I saw you last –
No words carry my experience.

Give me a chord, a verse
For this feeling
Or else a communion of voices sing out,
Our mouths are muted but my soul
Rejoices! Throat full of praise giving over
A solitude of worship.
You prepare a table and we break
Bread here – except there are no mingling hands,
And no shared cup.
Pull back the plastic. Give thanks.
A body of many parts, but these parts

Cannot touch. Hope is here,
Can you feel it?
Lift up your eyes, gather again,
Grieving world.

Suzanne Smith is a Scottish writer and library assistant, based in Edinburgh. She has a degree in English Literature from the University of Edinburgh and an MLitt in Postcolonial and World Literatures from the University of St Andrews. She reviews literary fiction on Instagram and is a regular contributor to *nb. Magazine*. Suzanne was part of the blogger tour that helped to promote Edinburgh Literary Salon's first anthology *Lost, Looking & Found*.

SPELL FOR COMFORT

Rosie Sumsion

The Word Witch was not who you thought she was. Firstly, she very rarely wore black. People just had a habit of visiting on laundry day when her usual wardrobe of soft jumpers was in the wash. Secondly, she was actually very fond of visitors, providing they were well-mannered. Most would find a cosy chair and discover that the only potion in the cauldron was (usually) Earl Grey tea. Finally, she did not have a cat. Instead, there was a gecko that could be found at the back of the bookshelves or on the warm hearth stones, and a deerhound with an inquisitive but polite nose. Luckily, the nose rarely strayed too far from the dog and could be reliably found investigating any visitor's plate of cake.

On this morning, the Word Witch was sitting by the window with a cup from the cauldron. Her gaze was fixed beyond the little garden to the far mountains, whose peaks were being tickled with tendrils of cloud. Her head was tangled. The words were slippery and falling out of place. Yes – it was time to go gathering. She hung the washing on the line, trusting the breeze to look after it while she was gone. She packed her bag and her lunch, and tied her boots. Then she and the dog (the gecko was staying home to mind the fire) closed the gate behind them and followed the path.

Soon they came to the river that would eventually wander down to the village. The Word Witch hung her socks and boots from her bag and splashed into the water. Despite the sun, the temperature still made her toes curl, and she barely felt the whisper of the fish that scurried for the shelter of the overhanging bank. She walked up the river for quite some time, the dog jumping in and out when he got too hot or too cold. She clambered up the short rapids and rolled up her trousers to wade through the deeper passes, where the banks were steep enough for ferns to lean over and play with her hair. In some places, the river widened to pebbly shallows where the current struggled to even graze her ankles. She followed the river until she understood where things began, then she climbed back out.

She sat on a rock and wriggled her toes in the sun, waiting for them to dry and warm up. The river had led her deep into the forest, to its heart, rarely visited by people. Consequently, a thick layer of moss carpeted the ground. It teemed with woodlice and other small insects navigating their own miniature forest. She followed the way they clambered and tumbled along invisible paths and noted what they carried with them. She traced their journeys into tree trunks and among the roots. She mapped where they met and separated again. She sat until her toes were dry and she knew how things connected, then she pulled on her socks and carried on.

By now, the sun was high overhead, but the overlapping leaves meant the Word Witch and her dog walked between flirting shadow and light. The dog's nose was investigating the scent of a squirrel (female, older, it suspected), and merrily led the little group between the trees. When the squirrel trail inevitably disappeared into the branches, the dog's nose quickly found a new one – this time sending them scrambling under bushes in search of a burrow.

'What a shame', thought both Word Witch and dog, 'that there are so many scents in the world, yet I have only one nose with which to smell them all.'

They followed the dog's nose under, over, and through the forest – dodging branches and delving into the undergrowth. They followed until the Word Witch knew what it was to be led. This meant it was lunchtime. She ate her sandwiches in a small clearing and finished with wild blueberries plucked from a thicket nearby. She wrapped some extras in her sandwich cloth and nestled them on top of her bag. They would be a reminder of surprising and special things as she ventured on.

Still with the fullness of lunch, the Word Witch came across a cave which she walked, then crawled, into, until the dark became liquid in its density. There she sat cross-legged until shades of grey revealed themselves, roughly sketching the shapes of the cave walls and larger boulders. She waited while the image was honed – fine shadows slowly mapping cracks, pebbles, and her own hands. Only when she could see what the darkness obscured did she re-emerge. The dog had quite sensibly decided to wait outside. Blinking in the light, she turned, only to find the darkness had already hidden its secrets again.

The cold has seeped into the Word Witch's bones; she

decides it is time to climb. Leaving her bag at the base of a tree trunk, she began to scramble from branch to branch. She felt the bark beneath her fingers and the way the smaller branches curved to hold her. Step by careful step she reached higher and higher, until she was able to pop her head out of the canopy and into the sunlight. She could see the hills that the clouds were now slithering down, beginning to pool at their bases. She could spot ribbons of silver where the river ducked in and out of the trees. Wisps of smoke from the village mingled in distant air with the smoke from her own chimney. The gecko must be working hard. The breeze made the tree gently sway, and birds surfed the current across the forest roof. The Word Witch closed her eyes and, for a moment, saw only pale pink as the sun warmed her face. She understood how bigger pictures can seem small, and clambered back down.

The dog, who had now done quite a bit of patient waiting, was happy to set off again. This time, they were beginning the journey out of the forest towards home. As they walked, the Word Witch began to weave. She twisted flexible branches into a circle and added young ferns that fanned outwards. She padded the inner rim with moss and lichen. Lastly, she added leaves, wildflowers, and the first, still green, autumn berries. It was a slow process, as she took only a little from each spot to ensure the forest would not miss anything. When it was finished, she hung it gently around the dog's neck like a collar. The reaching branches and layers of foliage created the impression of a great mane, as if she had befriended a curious forest lion. The Word Witch smiled to herself and knew what things can become.

They walked on like that – the Word Witch, the lion, and the dog's nose – down to the village. The villagers studied her black outfit and strange companion. They noted the dark clouds that were now weaving sly fingers through the forest from which she came. They looked to each other and saw mirrors of their own thoughts. They went home to make their plans.

Meanwhile, the Word Witch had reached her own home and already the wind was trying to bite her nose and fingers. She took the collar from the dog, thanking him for carrying it, of course, and hung it on the front door. Inside, she relieved the gecko of its duties and began to cook.

She sliced apples and tossed them with the blueberries to bake into a crumble, dusted with cinnamon. She rolled herbs, ham, cheese, and her own sundried tomatoes between pastry, and cut them into spiralled slices. She made fresh rolls, and dips studded with spices, which she dolloped into patterned bowls. She was just stirring the cauldron when there was a thump at the door.

Malcolm stood, a little damp, in the doorway, with a plate of biscuits balanced on one arm and her washing in the other. 'I thought I'd get it before the rain caught up,' he explained, then, glancing down at the rainbow puddle of clothes, 'Don't worry, I won't tell anyone!'

The Word Witch laughed and invited him in. Together they positioned every spare chair, pillow, and rug around the fire. Slowly, the villagers traipsed inside, submerging the tablecloth under the plates of food and leaving a line of shoes by the door. As people helped themselves and found places to sit, the storm too settled in. Eventually, when everyone was comfy and the dog had completed a thorough investigation of each plate, the Word Witch sat up straighter.

She thought about the river, and beginnings, and woodlice. She remembered the dark of the cave and the way the light had blinded her, and how things can change, or at least seem to. She imagined following her nose, or a path, or a hunch, and ending up somewhere new. She gathered all that she had collected in the forest and began:

'This story is not what you expect it to be…'

And outside, even the bawling wind and rain seemed to hold their breath – to lean in closer.

Rosie Sumsion is a third-year Social Anthropology and Social Policy student at the University of Edinburgh. Originally from the West Coast, she now lives in Edinburgh where she volunteers in local youth work and has worked with organisations such as Scottish Book Trust and the Edinburgh International Culture Summit. Rosie has always been a reader and is now switching speech-writing for fiction. She has a particular interest in children's books but is adamant that adults deserve just as much whimsy as the wee ones.

SPOON

Thomas Stewart

She was sure he was stealing the spoons. Sure enough that it began to annoy her, to really get to her – she started to take it personally. They felt like her spoons. She was sure enough that she decided to mention it to her colleague one day, only in passing, as if to test the water.

'He's stealing the spoons,' she said.

'Who, him?'

She could already tell by the tone of her useless co-worker that he wasn't going to believe her – nor would anyone else.

'He's weird, but harmless,' the co-worker went on.

The weird-but-harmless man always wore a green duffel coat, a pair of black-rimmed glasses, and carried a cane. It was hard to tell his age, he could be anywhere between forty and sixty and he always ordered a small cappuccino with cinnamon on the top instead of chocolate.

It started on a cold, rainy Wednesday, when the clouds lingered so long it was hard to tell what time of day it was, that she noticed the weird, harmless man was stealing the spoons. She saw it in the corner of her eye. Walking from the stockroom to the bar, she saw the old man take one of the small, silver teaspoons and plant it in his pocket. It was so quick she wasn't convinced it happened, to make sure, she turned around and they locked eyes. He stared through his glasses and she back at him before running off, unsure of anything. It rained that whole week and the man would come in every other day, sit alone for an hour or two, usually doing nothing but staring into blank space, appearing almost fulfilled by the sounds of other people talking. The week it rained, he stole four spoons, as far as she counted.

When it seemed like the rain would stop, the man walked past her, stomping his cane against the ground, as if to make a point. She listened carefully and was sure she heard the sound of clinking silverware. She named the man 'Spoon' from then on.

It was cheap, fake silver, of course. Spoon wasn't taking anything precious. But it was the principle behind it. She almost felt rejected, like she actually wanted to be part of his stealing spree and because of the silent rejection, she dreamed of catching him in the act, properly. Name and shame. Point and stare. Let all see the spoon stealer.

In her dreams, all the people stood and gasped, disgusted by Spoon's continuous betrayal – rejoicing only when the spoons were returned. She would be victorious.

She remembered handing over the thirteenth spoon. She held onto it for a second too long but it left her grip. Spoon glared at her before he took his cappuccino away. She felt too much like a co-conspirator – although she had entertained the idea of being part of it, this felt too far – like she had betrayed her cause. She spent most of her shift watching him. If he was going to take that spoon, she wanted to see it properly. And she didn't want to be alone. She was ready to alert anyone, to run to the cameras and check for proof. She was willing to ask him to empty his pockets.

When the queue stretched to the door and her manager barked orders at her, she stood at the coffee machine, frothing milk, adding syrup, her eyes on Spoon for as long as possible. But every time her head was down, she wanted it to be up. And that's when it happened. The minute she looked back up. Spoon stood and looked at her – right at her – as he slipped the small, sugar-coated spoon into his breast pocket. It seemed to happen in slow-motion, like he deliberately slowed himself down. And he left. And a customer was waiting impatiently for his drink, and she was too stunned that it had happened – that he looked at her as he did it – that she didn't say anything.

'Um, excuse me, Miss, can I have my one-shot decaf soya latte, please?'

After that day, Spoon's visits dwindled and it seemed his leg was getting better – he didn't limp as much. Once she saw him walking without the cane. He began coming twice a week. Then it was once a week – only on a Wednesday evening for a whole two months. And then it was nothing. Spoon seemed to vanish. By then he had claimed fifty-two spoons.

She had begun to make a list in her notebook, the date and time of each theft. But when he stopped showing up, she felt like he, himself, had been stolen. She knew nothing about him, had no way of finding him. She imagined him at another coffee house, betraying her.

Every night she thought about Spoon. And every night she became that bit more jealous of his disappearance. She fell asleep staring at empty suitcases.

A few days later, the woman arrived. Her hair was the colour of walnuts and she smelt of blackberries.

'May I speak to a manager?' the walnut woman said.

'I'm a manager,' she lied.

'I have something to confess and return.' Walnut produced three heavy bags-for-life full of spoons and placed them on the bar. 'My husband has a problem,' she said.

The sheer amount shocked her. She had miscounted, been looking down too long.

Walnut shook her head at herself. 'I cannot apologise enough. I've run them through the dishwasher twice. I am so sorry.'

'You don't have to apologise.'

'I do on behalf of my husband. He likes to take things and play characters. Did he show up with a cane?'

'Yes.'

'He doesn't need a cane. He ran a marathon last month. I am very sorry about the spoons.'

Suddenly, Walnut left and she was alone with the bag of spoons. Part of her wanted to preach the story to anyone who would listen – she was right all along. Right all along! But something stopped her. It might have been the three bags, or that nobody was around, but she said nothing and took the bags of spoons home.

Thomas Stewart is a Welsh writer based in Edinburgh. He has been awarded a New Writers Award from Scottish Book Trust and is the author of two pamphlets: *Based on a True Story* (Fourteen Poems, 2022) and *empire of dirt* (Red Squirrel Press, 2019). Thomas has an MA in Writing from the University of Warwick and was a writer in residence at Arteles, Finland. His work has been published in *Poetry Wales*, *Butcher's Dog, Best Scottish Poems 2019, The Amsterdam Quarterly, And Other Poems*, among others.

THE FISHERFOLK OF RAKHINE

Augustijn van Gaalen

For Aart Kooij, whose photographs
were the inspiration for this poem.

The day begins at four: when the sun is
  highest,
great bags of ice keep fish fresh
throughout the night: the beach, desolate and
  empty,
the shadows of nets waving
as heads submerge along the coast.

Dawn breaks and boats appear
sputtering, fish are brought to land
and arranged to dry on boiling sand.
Cigars are lit and smoked
as rounds are made from boat to shore
where women stand in half-moon formation:
baskets transferring from husband to wife.

At midday larger boats return
from open water: big-fish-land. Dragged along,
an endangered Manta weighs so much
that four men must harness the waves
to haul it ashore, where it is hacked to pieces
and loaded onto idling trucks, unsheathed.

When all the fish have gone, and the embers
blown to sea, there will be beer,
cigars, and bounties: of fish
rejoicing in the sea.

Augustijn van Gaalen is a Dutch writer and poet. His work has been published in *Gutter*, *Naugatuck River Review*, *Poetry Scotland*, and *Marble Poetry*, among others. He has an MA in Literature and Politics from the University of Glasgow.

WHEN THE POETS GATHER

Musenga Katongo

When the poets gather, when the writers meet
Words become handshakes and syllables greet
When the poets gather, when the griots sit
Stories become lessons and lessons become wit

When the poets gather, few give them chance
Because their writing doesn't make them dance
When the poets gather, when scribes start to
    think
They reflect on their deeds with words written in
    ink

When the poets gather, sadness takes stage
Happiness exits and reality jumps the page
When the poets gather, when the writers creep
Their words seep into minds and sink in deep

When the poets gather, when all hell breaks loose
Emotion and humour bond and forge a truce
When the poets gather, where the poets dwell
You will find weeping and laughter, and stories
    to tell.

Musenga Katongo is a Zambian award-winning spoken word artist, author, creative arts entrepreneur and founder of Colour Culture Arts. He is a four-time international and local poetry slam champion, TEDx Performer, and two-time award nominated author. Musenga won the Leith Versus the World Story Slam in June 2022, organised by the Edinburgh Literary Salon, and participated in the Edinburgh Festival Carnival, and Aye Festival.

HE FELL AMONG STORIES

David McVey

Colin struggled to remember how he'd got there, in that corner by the flashing lights of the Christmas tree, squeezed between two well-built women whom he understood were aunts. Not his aunts, but somebody's aunts, nevertheless.

'So anyway, he finds this cave, right?' a middle-aged man was saying. 'He'd been coming down the hill and he still had a ways to go before he got to the bus stop so he nips in the cave to get out of the rain. He's expecting the usual, drips from the roof, sheep dung, but instead it's like a palace – nae drips, high ceiling, carpets on the flair – and then he's stopped by these soldiers in tartan with muskets and swords and that.'

'Away!' said one of the aunts. The one on Colin's left.

'No, it's what he told me. He was a sober guy, my grandad, he didnae make stuff up. No often, anyway. So he says, who are you, and they say, we're the Jacobite Army. They say they're waiting there, in the wee cave thing, until the coast is clear and Bonnie Prince Charlie is ready again to get rid of the Hanoverians. And Grandad says, away, ye'd be two hundred years auld if ye were real

Jacobites and they say naw, it's only a few months since that Culloden business and Grandad says, ye'd better believe it, ye must have been sleeping for a long time. So he says tae them, come outside and I'll show ye how things have changed. He leads them out and as soon as they're outside and in the daylight they crumble away tae nuthin. Big pile of dust on the ground like someone's emptied a hoover bag.'

'Och, never,' said the aunt on his right.

'He told me. He wisnae kidding. He believed it.'

As the story ended, Colin remembered. Of course! It was when the satnav had started playing up – again – and had taken him off the M8 and into a long canyon-street of tenements with the lower storeys given over to pubs and bookies' shops and vaping companies and bargain grocers. He should have known better than to trust it.

As if there hadn't been enough mechanical failure for one day, the engine cut out just outside one of the bookies. These things, he thought, happen in threes. He tried to phone the AA. He had been meaning, for the last 100 miles, to plug his phone in to charge it. Now he couldn't, and the handset was lifeless.

He took a squint up and down the street. No sign of any telephone boxes. There were hardly any now, of course, and if you found one it probably just had a free lending library or a defibrillator inside.

'Ye awright, pal?'

He had partly wound down the driver window when the engine cut out, to prevent the windscreen steaming up, and a face appeared there now. A man had bent down to speak to him, a man who could be anywhere between thirty and sixty. He had several days' growth of stubble and wore a green beanie hat and a matching grey top and trackies.

'Not really,' he answered, all the same wondering if he really ought to admit weakness. He had heard about people driving off the freeway in Miami and ending up in dead-end neighbourhoods where they were murdered for their trainers. Was Glasgow like Miami? He must have been very obvious when he was struggling to start the car. Green hat had emerged from the entry door between the bookies and the pub next door. The man must have been watching and seen that Colin was stranded.

'Whit's the problem?'

'Three problems. My satnav got me lost, the car's broken down and my phone's out of charge.'

'No your day, is it?'

Colin couldn't help smiling. 'Is there anywhere I could phone the AA?'

'Well, there's nae AA box in this part of town. Somebody would only nick it. Ye can borrow my phone. It's a burner.'

'Thanks.' He stepped out of the car, locked it, took the offered phone and made the call while standing on the pavement. Racing commentary spilled out of the bookies' whenever anyone went in or out. In the middle of the call he asked green hat, 'Where is this?'

'Bailliecross,' said the man. 'This street's Steel Row.'

'Thanks.' He ended the call and handed the phone back. 'What do I owe you?'

'Och forget it. I'm a millionaire, so I am. How long are they gonnae be?'

'They said half an hour to an hour.'

'C'moan upstairs and have a cup of something. I saw

ye from the windae. Aa the family are gathered in there so I was standing there looking oot.'

He looked at the car, at the street, at the people going in and out of the bookies'. The man in the green hat seemed to read his mind. 'Och, naebody will nick it. They'll no even take the tyres. No if ye're parked outside the bookies. People have some respect.'

'If anyone wants to nick it he'll need a low-loader,' Colin smiled. He thought of his business partner, Greg. 'I've never been to Glasgow,' he'd said, 'but you know what they say. So stick to the main road, don't stop, keep the doors locked and the windows shut.'

And now his satnav had led him right into this unfamiliar Glasgow neighbourhood, the car was stopped and he was standing outside it.

'Yes, thanks, that would be great.' He heard himself responding to the invitation rather than consciously saying the words.

The stairs smelt of the pub downstairs and of polish and bleach. Greg would be surprised to learn that Glasgow people cleaned stuff. The man opened a first floor door – it wasn't locked – and led him inside. A short, carpeted lobby led into a cosy, noisy sitting room where a family party was in progress.

There were about a dozen people in the room, from a babe in arms to an ancient, toothless grandmother. A Christmas tree blinked in a corner between the two aunts and fake greenery and tinsel and plastic mistletoe hung from the walls. A middle-aged man was in mid-story. 'So he sobers up and finds himself in this toilet cubicle. He goes out and he's in the women's changing rooms at the sports centre…'

'Eh, here's the guy I saw,' said green hat, 'he's broke doon. Can we get him some tea and food and that?'

'Come in, come in, son,' said the middle-aged storyteller. 'Does he have a name, Gary?'

'Dunno,' said green hat. 'He's English.'

'I'm Colin. From Orpington.'

'Izzat a real place?' said a boy of about fourteen.

Introductions were made. The boy, Conor, was celebrating his birthday with his family ('It's rubbish having yer birthday this close to Christmas'). Green hat, Gary, was his father. Colin was handed a cuppa, cajoled into accepting a handful of custard creams and was squeezed in between the two aunts. The storyteller, now identified as Uncle Francis, continued. 'So there's all these naked and half-naked women spilling out of the showers and they see this man and there's this screaming and a manageress comes in and she goes up to Duncan and says she's gonnae call the polis and Duncan tells her, how dare you, madam, I identify as female and I will not tolerate such transphobic behaviour. Yes, please call the police, I wish to report you for your gender fascism. So he marches out and they leave him and then he legs it and manages to find a taxi. He made it to the wedding in loads of time.'

'They stag nights are awfy,' said the aunt on Colin's left, whom people referred to as Auntie May. She was a golden blonde woman in her fifties.

'How long does it take tae drive here from Orp-ing-ton?' asked Conor.

'Well, I left on Friday night after work. I stayed at a hotel in Peterborough, drove up to Edinburgh on Saturday to meet some clients and left there at two.'

'What business are ye in?' asked Francis.

'We sell refrigerator controls for food and drink businesses. I'm on my way to talk to people in the seafood industry in Oban.'

'Actually, at the moment,' said Gary, 'naw ye're no.'

'Och, Oban's lovely,' said Auntie May.

'Have ye been tae Glasgow before?' asked Conor.

'Er, no, first time.'

'Ye should spend time here. It's a great place. Well, no Bailliecross, but there's loads of great things tae see.'

'An aa the country roon aboot,' said Francis. 'The hills – the Kilpatricks, the Campsies, the Cathkin Braes, Tinto. Ye'll no have anything like them near Orpington.'

'Well, the Downs aren't too far away…'

'Talking of the Campsies,' said Francis, 'did I ever tell ye what happened to my grandad when he went walking in the Campsies one time?' And so the story had begun. Francis's grandad in the Campsie Fells, the rain starting and his taking refuge in a cave and his encounter with the shades of the Jacobite Army.

'Ye're an auld twister, Francis,' said the old woman, the first time Colin had heard her speak.

'Naw I'm no. But my grandad might have been.'

'What happened to the cave?' asked Conor. Most of the adults smiled.

'He went back there loads of times,' said Francis, but he never found it again.'

'I bet he didnae,' said a woman they called Mary, who appeared to be Conor's mother.

The old woman, a grandmother, the grandmother of most of them, perhaps, said, 'It's no a good thing tae be broke doon.'

'No,' Colin agreed. 'It's not.'

'Erchie once hired a car. We'd tae go tae a wedding in Inverness. The trains were off because of the snow so I asks him how he thinks he's gonnae get a car through and he says by no drivin on the railway line. Men!' She and all of the other women laughed.

'When was this?' asked May.

'Och, forty or fifty year ago. I cannae remember exactly. Anyway, the road was different then, narrower and winding and wi steeper climbs. And of course whit dae we no dae but break doon? Somewhere after Blair Atholl, complete middle of naewhere. Turns oot the road's shut ten miles further on anyway.'

'It's just selfish getting married somewhere daft like Inverness in the winter,' said the aunt who wasn't May.

'So ye were lucky ye didnae go any further, Maw?' said Francis.

'Naw, no really, son. There wis nae traffic – everybody else had listened tae forecasts on the wireless, no like yer dad. But at least we'd just passed one of they AA boxes so yer dad went and phoned from it. He said the guy almost burst oot laughing at the idea of being called oot on a night like that. He's just about tae suggest we walk back along the road and see if we can reach Blair Atholl and maybe find a wee bed and breakfast and then we see a light off the road tae the one side. Well, there must be a hoose over there so we start through the snow, sprachling up tae our knees, dragging our bags. Sure enough there's a wee cottage and we bang on the door of the porch and this smelly wee Highland guy gets out. He says they already have an important guest but we say we're no guests we're just folk caught in the snow and we need tae stay somewhere warm. So he leads us past this sitting room where this auld woman dressed in black is being waited on by what look like servants and by the wee Highland guy's wife. He shows us into this room with a pallet bed and brings us some oatcakes, cheese and some milk. When we're alone I say to yer dad, did ye see her, all in black, just like her photies, and he's saying, away, woman, nonsense.

'We wake up next morning freezing and see there's nae roof and the snow is landing on us and we're just lying on some rotten planks of wood. The rest of the hoose is just a shell as well. There's naebody aboot.'

'Had it been hit by a navalanche?' asks Conor.

'We got back tae the car,' she said, ignoring Conor, 'and the AA man gets there just after us. He fixes the car a treat – it's something dead simple – and tells us the road north is still blocked so we should just drive back home. He points to the ruin of the cottage and say we're in good company getting stuck in the snow oot here. He says that's Victoria Cottage. The story goes that Queen Victoria was on a Highland tour and got caught in the snow and had tae be put up for the night by the poor folk that lived there. I says tae yer Dad, did I no tell ye it was her?'

There came a sudden hooting outside. Gary looked out of the window. 'Talk o the devil – it's yer AA man.'

Colin thanked them all and they wished him Merry Christmas and a Happy New Year.

Two hours later Colin had just driven past a village called Tyndrum in snow-clogged darkness. There was little traffic on the road and at one point a train swept by, away from Oban, looking like the last train ever from anywhere. Colin found himself wondering if the Bailliecross people had been real, or something like the ghost of Queen Victoria. Perhaps they were wondering the same about him, and Conor was Googling to see if Orpington was a real place.

The snow grew heavier. There were still no other cars. Colin really hoped he wouldn't break down again.

David McVey lectures at New College Lanarkshire. He has published over 120 short stories and a great deal of non-fiction that focuses on history and the outdoors. He enjoys hillwalking, visiting historic sites, reading, watching telly, and supporting his hometown football team, Kirkintilloch Rob Roy FC. He is a frequent visitor to Edinburgh and, in his non-fiction work, has written widely about its history, cityscapes and literary heritage.

GATHERING

Fiona Herbert

*Thank you for choosing us for your order of service. We are
sorry for your loss. Please now gather the photographs and
text you wish to be included.*

Before your scattering, I had three days
to gather and distill your life
from fragments.
I bundled all I found in bags and boxes.

You had kept so much unborn:
your poems, a note of what to say next time
   you saw me
crumpled among P60s since 1963.

Beneath completed crosswords to *The Times*,
lay drafts of longed-for letters, never sent, and
   scrawl;
I gathered every sacred scrap.

Gifts from your children still in cellophane –
   I turned away
to bulging pouches crammed in chocolate boxes
where photographs slipped out:
you at twenty, handsome, suited, smiling
   shyly;

me, a toddler, sullen and cagouled
on a holiday that nobody remembers.
You with cheerful strangers, raising amber
    pints in toast
or rueful, on a drizzly hill.
A hundred unmarked landscapes.

A birthday card I made you.
A list of resolutions
or promises? Unsure.

*The property will be cleared once we have received your
instruction to proceed. Please ensure any items you wish
to keep have been removed.*

And what of your belongings? What to
    gather?
A clatter of cassettes, defunct, creak-hinged
    in their scuffed plastic
I let them go
(but noted names, for future reference)
I kept all your vinyl, yet to play.

A small tin ship; I'll never know where from
    now.
A globe I gave you.
A gluggle jug you washed my hair with
just that one time.

The sagging shelves of books. I kept them all.
Your soft old wallet. Your tired walking boots.

I left your stark flat, hoping I had gathered all
   I needed,
hoping you would follow, and scatter into
   sunlight.
Hoping I had not gathered more than I could
   hold.

Fiona Herbert is a writer, oral storyteller and editor, who has attended the Edinburgh Literary Salon for over a decade. She loves both poetry and prose, and enjoys creating feminist retellings of traditional tales in her storytelling performances. Her fiction writing often uses elements of myth and folklore as a springboard for other ideas. When not prancing about telling stories or helping other writers through her editorial work, she continues her own works-in-progress – currently a novel for children about the Cailleach, and a novel for adults about the Corryvreckan whirlpool.

GATHERING FOR ADVENTURE

Roddie McKenzie

You watch the clock crawling round to 9am. They will be starting to gather under the carved tree; it's time to go. The jaggy tummy feeling lifts you out of the chair on to your feet. When Granpa asks you if you were going to waste the day cluttering up his kitchen, he sends a huge puff of blue-grey smoke up to the ceiling as he taps his cigarette ash into a saucer, and turns on the transistor radio. With his grey beard and the rising smoke, he looks like a wizard. You feel that he can read your mind, you shake your head.

'No, Granpa, I'm going out.'

'Where to?'

You feel the heat and guilt rise to your face. How does he know? Your own words seem to come from far away.

'Uh, nowhere special – just meeting Jenny, Morag, and Gordy. Maybe we will walk round the island, so I won't be in at dinnertime.'

'What about your dinner?'

It seems to take an eternity for you to answer, but you hear yourself say: 'I have my pocket money, so I can buy a roll and juice at Fintry Bay cafe.'

This seems to satisfy him, and he turns back to the pots he's putting away.

'Well, I'm making your favourite – Eve's Pudding – for the guests, be back on time for tea if you want some.'

'I will, thanks Granpa… bye.'

That song 'Sugar, Sugar' comes on the radio as you rush out of the kitchen. It's by the The Archies. You wonder how cartoon characters can get a song to number one in the charts.

You head up over the high, back green of Mansewood, Gran and Granpa's boarding house. It once was a manse for the Wee Frees, with a big garden in which Granpa grows vegetables for the kitchen. Pausing at the hedge around the high green vegetable border, you recover the tin and rattle it. Great, they're still there! Stuffing it in your anorak pocket, you climb up the hand holds on the back wall, scramble over the whinstone slab coping, and dreep into the Cowbrae.

The summer holiday sun is hot, so you take off the anorak and tie it round your waist by its arms. The Cowbrae is like a green tunnel, with some open bits where you can see horses in the field overlooking the Cathedral. The gorse is yellow on the roller-coaster Sheuchan hills. You see them from your back bedroom window in the boarding house; it's such a better horizon than the tenements from your bedroom window at home in the city.

The hedges of the Cowbrae bend like a banana up and down the crest of the little hill of Tor Mor before descending downhill to the new houses. You run down the last section to where the lane comes out at the new council houses. Your Cumbrae cousins are waiting for you under the big ash tree, where you all carved your initials last summer.

You love summers in Millport and wish you lived here, with the un-smelly air, clear skies, hills, and seashore, a short walk out the door. It feels unfair that they live here, and you live in the smoky, noisy city. When you were younger, at the end of the holiday when Ma and Da came down to take you home, you and your cousin, Jenny, would run away in an attempt to miss the last boat to Fairlie, where you would board the puffing train back to the city. It never worked – the pair of you were not smart enough to stay off the main streets and you never thought that there would just be another paddle steamer calling the following morning.

Gordy is twelve, two years older than everyone, and he is the leader.

'Did you get the matches, Davy?'

'Yes, Gordy,' you reply.

'Did you get the bacon, Morag?'

'Aye, Gordy.'

'Jenny – frying pan, breid, tatties?'

'Yeah, Gordy, in my duffel bag.'

'Is any yin a fearty? Any yin want to back out of the expedition to the Forbidden Hills?'

We eye each other before shaking our heads.

'Okay let's go then.'

We take the fields behind the houses to avoid anyone who might spot us and ask questions or pass on news of us. All the grown-ups gossip in this wee town… and there are some wee clipes too.

We come out on the Ferry Road, at the bottom of the Farland Hills. They rise up through the woodland to the mountain top. It's like Kanchenjunga that you read about in *Swallows and Amazons*. It got everyone talking about the trip, but here you are at the base of the Farlands, steeper, with more cliffs than the Sheuchans and forbidden by the grown-ups. A day ago, we met and agreed to break that rule after seeing that black-and-white film on the telly about explorers in the jungle. Now, at the marshy bit at Farland Point, you gaze at the Farlands' big red cliffs that go straight up.

We find the way with little problem; our uncles and parents have taken us up through the woods to the moor, but never over the tops to the edge of the cliff. They said that if you stand on the edge of the grass, it would move like a conveyor belt and slide underneath you, sending you off the cliff, screaming, to your death.

Puffing and panting, we reach the top of Craigengour; the view is amazing – the blue grey Clyde all the way down to the Ailsa Craig, the pointed rocky mountains of Arran, and across the orange sands of Kames Bay, the ferry Keppel making for the Old Pier with a white trail behind. Winds whip across the top. To get out of the wind, you go down to a little circular den made from rocks for the sheep. Gordy tells you to help him haul a big flat piece of stone to make the fire on. He takes out a jack knife with a saw on it, to cut dry gorse to start the fire. He sends you to the edge of the wood to find dry branches. You give him the tin with the matches, but he lets you light one edge of the kindling, as he calls it. You want to throw on the sticks as the flames crackle, but he tells you to slow down, or you'll smother it.

When the fire is blazing, Jenny takes the frying pan and the bread wrapped in a waxy Mothers Pride paper from her duffel bag. She borrows the jack knife and cuts the tatties into thin slices, then throws the bacon into the pan and the fat oozes out, sizzling. She adds the tatties.

Gordy pulls out a bottle of limeade from his haversack, you watch how he releases the cap little by little.

'So it doesn't fizz over after being shoogled aboot on the climb up,' he says. You nod and learn.

Jenny howks the bacon and golden-brown tattie slices out of the pan onto the bread. The drops of fat glisten on the white bread, making the little holes look bigger. You blow on the tatties and bacon, the whole den smells like Sunday morning and the taste is... supercalifragilistic-expialidocious! The bottle is passed around and you all slug the limeade.

After a while Gordy says, 'Who dares tae go tae the cliff wi me?'

Your stomach tingles, but you put up your hand – so does Morag.

'Okay, you twa, follow me, do whit ah say.'

You both follow him downhill to where the land stops before the sky. He edges forward and peers over the edge. He pauses then moves back.

'Stand here – on the rock – not on the loose stuff, or the grass.'

You edge forward, expecting the edge to slip away at any moment, and look down. It is like looking out the window of Derek's new hoose in the multis in Whitevale street, back in Glesga. Except instead of cars, you are looking onto the tops of trees and the coastal road, wiggling like the snake it looks like on the map, beyond your black sandshoe at the edge of the rock.

The scary bit is over, you are a hero, you run back to the shelter as Morag steps forward. Jenny is scouring the pan with grass before putting it back in her duffel bag. From the top of Craigengour, you all head north to look at the Druid Stone in the wood beyond the farm.

You are all pirates on the path down, chopping down redcoat musk thistles with your stick swords (it's okay to chop those ones, but not the spear thistles, which are, says Gordy, 'our country's emblem'). There are hundreds of redcoats and they keep coming, but we fight our way down the long sloping ridge. We are all sworn by an oath to secrecy. The grown-ups were wrong when they said you'll fall and die. You realise that they use little white lies to control kids. All the time.

Your company parts at the new houses. It is quarter to five and you skip back up the Cowbrae to Mansewood, sneaking in by the secret way over the back wall.

The Eve's pudding tastes better than ever.

Roddie McKenzie lives in Dundee and is a member of Wyvern Poets and chairman of Nethergate Writers. He has published short stories in Nethergate Writers anthologies since 2006 and recently his poetry and prose have appeared in: *Tether's End Magazine, Lallans, Seagate III, New Writing Scotland 35, Northwords Now 36, 50 Shades of Tay, Writers Cafe Magazine 16* and in the Scottish Book Trust book, *Rebel*. Previously, he was a Senior Lecturer at the University of Edinburgh and graduated with an MBA from Edinburgh University. He lived in 'Auld Reekie' for eight years.

KITCHEN LOVE, PART ONE

Naomi Head

(After Ella Risbridger)

My greatest stories start in the kitchen
and my greatest loves,
have been kitchen loves.
Domestic loves.
Easy, buttery kinds of love.

My old flatmate
is one of the great loves of my life.

I fell in love with her in a kitchen,
our old kitchen, at 2am.
While I was pouring boiling water onto loose
    leaf tea,
and she was making toast.

We often made tea in our teapot,
and toast with the toaster
which lightly burned smiles into the bread.
Not obvious companions to our windowsill chats,
but necessary comforts
for revealing secrets.
We were both lost in those days.
And it was in that kitchen,
we fell in love completely.

By love, I mean everything you think,
I mean domestic, easy, buttery love.
The kind of love you can spread evenly on toast.

I hated when we were separated,
because this ritual brought together
our two halves and made a whole.

There are a million kinds of love,
as many as there are people to fall in love with,
And a million more ways to love a person.
But sometimes love is domestic,
and easy and buttery.

I never told her this.
She already knew,
because we made each other
five thousand pots of tea.
We brewed something domestic,
something easy and buttery.
We brewed intimacy.
We brewed love.

Naomi Head is a writer and poet based in Edinburgh. Her work explores her relationships with food, friends and family. She also uses writing to process her mental health challenges and emotions. Her poetry has been published by Sunday Mornings at the River, Scran Press, SNACK Mag and Beyond the Veil Press, and shared online by I AM LOUD and the Spit it Out Project.